Great Feminization!

MILFS, lactation, sisters who feminize, body swapping, and more!

Breaking a Man In!

The Jamaican Sex Change!

Feminized by a Lactating MILF!

Feminized by Two Sisters!

The Feminization of Jack!

Grace Mansfield

ISBN: 9798874009724

TABLE OF CONTENTS

NOVELS BY GRACE MANSFIELD AND ALYCE THORNDYKE

My Husbands Funny Breasts
Too Tough to Feminize
I Changed My Husband into a Woman
The Emasculation Project
The Feminization Games
A Woman Unleashed
The Stepforth Husband
Revenge of the Stepforth Husbands
The Sissy Ride
Feminized by a Ghost
The Curse of the Werefem
Silithia
The Big Tease
Womanland
The Man Who Abused a Woman
A Woman Gone Mad
Sissy Slaves the Book
The Once and Future Man
The Day the Democrats Turned the Republicans
The Broken Man
Breaking Jack
Monastery of Broken Men
Ship of Broken Men
The Horny Wizard of Oz
The Lusty Land of Oz
Hucows, Bully Boys and Were-Cows
the Sissy Transition
I was Feminized and Dominated!
Toy for a Sex Monster!
Femwood Mansion!
Female Different!
Sex Crazy!
The Long, Hot Feminization!
Fade to Pink!

You can find bundles and collections at

https://gropperpress.wordpress.com

A Note from the Author!

Got five lovelies for you!

Tom gets caught eating his own cum, and that starts a journey he never expected!

Dave went limp and the doctor says go on vacation. A little voodoo and he and his girlfriend are really relieving the stress!

Rod's fascination with lactation sends him down the pink path!

Gary cheated, and now he has to pay the price…double!

Jack's wife plays a joke on him that leads to feministic extremes!

Are you ready? Dig in and have the time of your life!

STAY HORNY!
Gracie

Breaking a Man In!

Feminization, chastity and pegging go a long way!

Grace Mansfield

A Note from the Author!

Men are so silly. They walk around and swagger so tough, and they are putty in a real woman's hands.

Take the case of Tom, he was living life, acting like a man, and, suddenly, his world changes.

And it took nothing but a subtle, little plan that anybody could do… if they were as clever as a woman!

A plan that included chastity, pegging, and, of course, feminization!

Read on, reader, and…

STAY HORNY!

Gracie

Part One

Tom stared at the computer screen.

On the screen Wifey was slurping away on a big, huge penis. It was as big as her head, and she could only get half of it in her mouth.

She sucked, and she fondled big, huge balls, and she watched as the man in a mask groaned and came closer and closer.

Tom was breathing harder and harder, and his hand was doing some fondling of its own. A healthy dose of oil made his knob super shiny and he twisted his palm over the head and stroked the shaft.

He wasn't as big as the fellow doing Wifey's mouth, but he was big enough.

Suddenly Wifey stood up and pushed the masked man back on the bed. He stared up at her, and she climbed up over his body, placed her snatch directly over him and descended.

"Oh, fuck!" Tom whimpered. He was feeling it. He could feel the cum boiling in his nuts. He could feel it surging and starting to push up the shaft.

On the monitor Wifey rocked back and forth, the masked man's huge dong sliding back and forth, in and out, and he grunted, "I'm gonna... I'm gonna..."

The white squirtem shot up Tom's shaft and he grunted as white white took over his mind. He cupped his hand in front of his penis so he wouldn't make a mess.

Jan would nag him mercilessly if she knew he masturbated!

But, damn! A guy needs it! And Jan had been feeling a little punk and hadn't given it to him, so he...he...

On the screen white ropes slapped across Wifey's face, made her red lips shiny, and she blinked at the force of the ejaculation.

At the exact same moment, duplicating to the second the thrusts and jerks of the masked man on the screen, Tom lurched and jerked and white fluid—-

"Honey! I'm home!"

Tom couldn't stop the semen filling his palm.

He also couldn't stop the click, click, click of Jan's heels coming down the hall.

"Tom?"

She was only a few feet away from seeing him, his pants unzipped and his hand full of cum!

"Honey?"

He tried to do several things at once. He shoved forward, trying to get his swivel, and his naked cock, into the kneehole under his desk; he tried to move the mouse with his left hand, across the keyboard, and close the browser window; he slapped hie right hand to his mouth.

He had no choice!

He felt his hot seed thrust into his mouth and he licked his palm, and then brought his hand down.

"Hey, honey. Guess who I ran into?"

Tom smiled with a closed mouth. The stuff was salty and he wanted to throw up, but he kept his mouth shut and gulped.

It slid down his throat, it was like swallowing snot, but, oddly, not disgusting.

It tasted good. Salty with a hint of sweet.

He blinked rapidly at his wife.

"Ta da!"

His wife's friend from college, Donna, stepped into the room.

They had been walking in synch, two sets of heels sounding as one.

"Hi, Tom!"

"Um…uh…wow!" He tried to talk with a closed mouth, working his mouth and trying to swallow. It felt like it was all gone, but…but…the guilt was totally in his mind.

He couldn't stand up, he couldn't show that his penis, still hard, was hitting the top of the kneehole. He couldn't let them see the slick slime slathered all over his glans.

"Hi!" opening his mouth very slightly.

"I went to the local Starbucks and she came in right after me! After five years, and we run into each other."

"It's like fate!" Donna blurted.

"Uh, yeah! That's…oh, sorry. I can't get up to greet you. Got a cramp."

The two women stood at the door, happy as clams, and they were a beautiful pair. Jan was a blonde and Donna was a redhead. Both were stacked, and they looked an awful lot like sisters.

"Oh, don't get up. I'll come to you."

Donna rounded the desk and bent down to give him a hug, and she saw everything. She saw his pants open, his weenie now in a half a chub, traces of semen all over the head of his cock.

Tom turned eighteen shades of red. His eyes revealed his shame, but Donna didn't blink. She did smile a bit, and she kissed him, right on the mouth, and then she did react. A moment of surprise, and she jerked back. Then she recovered.

"It's so good to see you."

"We're going to make some drinks. Come out when you can."

Tom nodded, and Donna partially blocked Jan's view of him. Blocked the sight of his red face, the panic crossing his face, the embarrassment.

Donna backed up six inches, was facing Tom, and she chirped, "Yes. Join us, Tom. We've got a lot to talk about."

It was a threat, plain and simple. It was in her eyes, in her smirk, in the way she looked at him.

"Uh…okay."

Then the two girls were gone, walking down the hall, now their heels clicking not in harmony, more like a herd of tap dancers.

Tom couldn't breath.

She had seen him. She had seen his cock. She knew he had been jacking off.

Oh, fuck!

On the other hand, she hadn't told Jan. She hadn't pointed at his groin and exclaimed, "Your dick is out! And it just squirted! Oh, my God!"

Instead, she had made it a secret, kept just between them.

He quickly wiped his penis off and pushed it back in his pants, zipped up and buckled.

Then he reached over for the bottle of water he kept on his desk, and his hand stopped.

He could taste the unique taste of semen in his mouth.

He had never tasted his own semen before.

Oh, he had thought about it. When he was younger, before he was married, he had even tried to squirt in his own mouth. He had put his back to the wall, his butt in the air and his neck bent under him.

He had jerked and jerked, exhilarated and terrified at the same time, but when he finally shot his load he aimed away and clamped his mouth shut.

He just couldn't.

But now, an accident, he had. He had tasted, and swallowed, a full load of cum.

A tablespoon of the stuff, over the tongue and sliding down his throat.

And…he liked it.

Naughty and nasty and tasty and…he couldn't believe that it tasted so good.

Funny, he had read stories, porn stories, where women claimed to like the taste of sperm more than they liked to screw, and he had thought that was just…not true.

But now that he had actually sampled himself…my God!

Why did women even bother with regular sex? Why didn't all women just give blowjobs!

Tasty and nutritious, and no mess dripping out of their holes!

He sat and stared at the computer and his mind wandered over all the implications.

He liked the taste of cum. Better than ice cream. And he was going to do it again. There was no doubt about that.

Then he heard the tap of heels in the hallway.

"Oh, crap! He had no intention whatsoever of going out to have a drink with the girls. He was going to hide in his office until Donna left! He was going to—

Donna entered the room. She was holding two glasses and had a big grin on her face.

"You were under orders to come out for a drink."

Tom's tongue was befuddled. He didn't know what to say, but he fumbled the beginnings of an excuse.

"Yeah, uh, sorry. I've got a lot of, uh, work to—"

Donna rounded the desk, placed the two glasses on the table to the left of the desk, and bent over him. She reached right down into his groin.

She kissed him soundly, and then she was doing something with his mouth…she was licking the insides!"

"Mphpph! Wha—"

She went back, squatted on her heels, and looked at him.

"I knew it. I tasted cum in your mouth. And your dick was out. And it was slimy. We walked in on you eating your own cum."

"No! No! I wasn't!" He was begging and blathering, his voice low so Jan wouldn't hear it. She was all the way in the kitchen, but he as still scared.

And he was scared that Donna might blab.

"Give it up, Tommy Boy. I know what cum tastes like. I also know that when a man squirts he can't get it up for a while."

Her hand shot down to his groin and she grabbed him.

He tried to back away, but the swivel chair was caught, and his hands were on the desk, and he couldn't stop her.

He held his dong through his pants and waited.

"Stop it! Please!" His eyes were filling with water.

And waited. "Nope. You shot your load and there's nothing left."

"Let me go," he sobbed.

She did. Then she licked her fingers and wiped at his mouth. Her lipstick came off.

"Don't want Jan to see this. She might get the wrong idea. After all, you're not a cheater, you're just an onanist."

"Donna, you can't tell her!"

"Hey, honey, it's okay. I'm an onanist, too. See, we've got something in common. Of course, if you really don't want me to tell Jan that you masturbate and eat your own cum, you're going to have to do something for me."

"Anything! No, wait! What do you mean?"

"Hey, just relax. Now, we've got to go out and act natural and normal. You've got to come out and have a drink with us. Here, drink this one, compose yourself, and come out."

She put a drink in his hand, bourbon and Coke, and he needed a drink. He took it, looked at it, looked at her, then gulped rapidly.

"That's a boy." She picked up her drink and went back around the desk.

"Wait! What are you…what did you mean? What do I have to do for you?"

She was at the door. She turned to him. Her left hand came up to her breast, hefted it, pointed it at him, and her right hand tilted her glass.

Then she smiled, "I'll let you know. Now come out here. You've got exactly one minute to get your sexy butt out here. And remember, act like nothing has happened.

She turned and walked down the hall, and Tom heard her say, "He'll be right here. He was just finishing something…" her voice faded, became two voices chattering excitedly.

Tom tilted his glass and sucked that bourbon down like he was a drunk.

But he wasn't a drunk, he was just desperate.

Holding the glass in tight fingers, he got up and headed down the hall.

Tom sat in a club chair and watched the two women talk.

Gawd, what a pair of lookers.

If he hadn't just squirted he would have been bonerized up the yin yang!

But he had.

And the looks from Donna kept reminding him of that.

She was subtle, just a glance, presumably to keep him in the conversation, but the knowing look in her eyes…he was totally busted.

Yet she didn't say anything, which was weird.

She was the kind of woman who was snide and played 'one up,' and enjoyed busting men's balls.

But, damn, she was good looking.

"Isn't that wonderful, dear? Donna gets to stay with us for three weeks!"

"Huh? What?" He was jerked out of his daydreaming.

"She's taking a class for her work and she's going to be in town for three weeks. We've got the spare bedroom, and…"

"Oh, I couldn't do that!" murmured Donna, but it was obvious that this was probably her plan the whole time. Running into his wife 'accidentally.' Hunh!

"Nonsense. We've got the room, and we can spend all your spare time drinking and partying."

They giggled.

"But is it all right with Tom?" Donna looked directly at him, and the look was in her eyes. *Say 'yes' or I'll tell your wife about the cum you've been eating.*

"Of course it is. Tell her, Tom."

Tom didn't want to. He didn't want manipulating and conniving in his house for three weeks, let alone a single day!

But, he was caught. "Uh, yeah. Sure."

"See? He hesitates. He doesn't really want the company, and—"

"Tom! Tell her and don't hesitate."

Now the look was in his wife's eyes. *Say 'yes' or you're not going to get any sex for a year!* And, in fact, he knew she would try to make him wear that stupid chastity device. The 'toy' that wasn't a toy. The device that he hated and she loved.

So he didn't hesitate. "Sure, it would be great. It would be an excuse to drink some bourbon." *A lot of bourbon!*

"See? We're going to have a wonderful time!"

"Well, okay. But…are you sure?"

"Of course we are. Aren't we Tom?"

And so the wolf stepped into the middle of the sheep.

It was bad from the very first day. Donna had her luggage at a hotel and Tom was drafted to help her move her suitcases. And it wasn't just the suitcases.

"Tom will drive you over and help you with your luggage. And, say, you can even use his car while you're here!"

Tom opened his mouth to object, but the look Jan cast him stopped him in his tracks.

Didn't his wife see what kind of a person her friend was?

But she didn't, and she didn't because, Tom had to admit, his wife had the same type of personality. Not glaring, but she was guilty of the occasional manipulation herself.

So he drove Donna across town in his classic 1966 Chevy Malibu.

The Malibu was his pride and joy, and he didn't want anybody to drive it.

"You'll be careful, won't you?"

She was sitting next to the window and suddenly slid over next to him. Her hand dove into his groin and grabbed him. "Oooh, you've got a boner again."

"Urk! Let go!"

"Nonsense. Every man likes his dingus handled. Just consider this my way of paying you room and board."

He held the wheel with his left and hand and tried to brush her hand away with his right, but she had a grip on him.

She snuggled up against him, pressed her boobs against his fight arm and quipped, “Isn’t this fun? It’s just like we’re on a date in high school.”

“But I’m married!” he begged.

“Don’t worry, Tommy Boy. You won’t be hitting any home runs on me. You’ll be getting to first base a lot, though.

“Please! I don’t want to be untrue to Jan!”

“Why do you eat your own cum, anyway?”

“Oh, God!” She was rhythmically opening and closing her grip, and he felt the thrill of the groin obscuring his mind.

“Come on. Tell me.”

“It was an accident!” he blurted.

“Right!” she laughed. “I can see the headline…man accidentally eats his own cum.”

“I didn’t expect you guys…and I came just when you got home and you came into my office and I didn’t know what to do!”

“So you hid the evidence. Well, very clever. How’d you like it?”

“I didn’t!” he lied.

“I don’t believe that. As I said, I like masturbating, and I love licking my fingers. And I’ve sucked a lot of men, and I love the taste. And a couple of times I’ve done snowballs, you know what a snowball is?”

He shook his head and wished she’d let go of him.

“It’s when a woman sucks a man off, then French kisses him, transferring all that lovely cum into his mouth.”

“Oh…ew!” He tried to mock up disgust, but now he was thinking.

“I’d like to do that to you. Suck on your hog until you blew your load, then give you a big, old sloppy…wow! Your ding dong is going wild!”

“That’s because you’re squeezing it!”

“I doubt that. You’re a kink, Tom, and I just found out.”

He groaned, and it was all he could do to not hump her hand, it felt that good.

Fortunately, they arrived at the hotel.

She was on the ground floor and she led the way into her room, closed the door and took off her clothes.

“Wait! What are you doing?”

“I need a shower. I didn’t have time this morning.”

“No! Wait! You can take one back at the house! You can jump in the pool!” *And drown!* he thought.

“But this is more fun,” she chuckled, watched his eyes as she shed her blouse and revealed her humongous breasts. She wiggled out of her skirt, was aware of how Tom licked his lips and couldn’t stop himself from staring at her.

"How long, Tom. How long has it been since you got yourself some strange pussy?"

"Please, stop," he was almost crying. "I don't want to do this."

She moved into him, pressed her body against his and placed her hands on his cheeks. "I told you, you're not going to. But I'm going to have some fun with you."

She kissed him. His hands were trying to stave her off, but she had a hold of his package. Hell, she had his package in a death grip! She mashed her mouth against his, then backed off and licked his lips. He could taste the slightly sweet taste of her lipstick. He could feel the waxy texture.

"Woo! That's fun. Aren't stolen cookies great?"

She turned and sauntered into the bathroom. As she reached the doorway she turned and looked coquettishly back at him, "Just play with yourself for a moment, eh, lover?"

Tom stood, frozen, and heard the water start up in the shower.

He wiped his mouth, hoping he got everything, he didn't want his wife to suspect anything.

He sat on the bed, next to her open suitcase, and stared at her lingerie.

It was on top of her clothes, and he stared at the big cups. Oh, Lord. It wouldn't be so bad if she wasn't so sexy!

Five minutes later she stepped out of the shower. She stood in the bathroom, in front of the mirror, and dried her hair.

Tom couldn't help staring through the open door at her milky skin, her sloping breasts, the way she quickly refreshed her make up.

She came into the bedroom, a nude goddess, and smiled at him as she got dressed.

She glanced at his groin and grinned. "Still hard, eh? Good."

"You can't do this to me. I'm a happily married man."

"I love happily married men. I'm always stuck with horny types that want to screw and run. I'd like to get a man who just wants to snuggle and screw all night long."

"You're evil," he muttered miserably.

She laughed. "Oh, you have no idea."

A half hour later, after a boner fondling ride back across town, Tom carried Dona's luggage into the guest room. He couldn't believe how hard he was. He had just masturbated the day before, but her continual attentions were wreaking havoc with his sex.

"Oh, good! You're back!" And the two women went on with their eternal blathering.

Tom headed for his office. He had to work. He had to take his mind off this situation. He had no idea how he was going to last two weeks.

That night they had a small celebration dinner to welcome Donna. Tom grilled steaks on the patio and the girls sat on lounge chairs and sipped Vodka martinis and observed his ass.

"Now take Tom's ass, for instance. It's round, and good looking, but is it hard?"

"It's not his ass that I want to be hard," giggled Jan.

"Yes, but he has to have the hammer to drive the nail. Does he have a muscular fanny? Or is it just a slothful, flabby, butt."

"It's pretty muscular." Then Jan leaned over and whispered into Donna's ear. "At least it is when I grab his buns and pull him into me."

Both girls were a little tipsy now, and they laughed hysterically.

Tom had heard the remark, and he chose to ignore it. All day long the girls had been like this. Secretive and teasing and making quips that were, if not embarrassing, then humiliating.

He flipped the steaks and sipped some bourbon and Coke. How could those bitches stand vodka? Were they communists or something?

"I want to feel his butt."

"Tom! Come here!"

"Oh, no! I'll burn the meat."

"I'll burn your meat!" threatened Jan. Her humor was lost on him.

"Come on, sweet cheeks. We need to do a comparison test."

"No!"

They came to him. He heard their chairs squeak, their feet pattering, then their hands were feeling his ass.

"Hey!"

They were on both sides of him, Donna on the left, Jan on the right, and they were pressing against his arm with their breasts.

Each grabbed a butt cheek and squeezed.

Tom would have jumped, but they were weighing him down.

"He is hard."

"He's hard in front, too. Feel him."

"Really?"

"Oh, yes."

"Stop it," gurgled Tom as Donna ran her hands right under his belt. "Oh, Lord, you weren't kidding! Feel this big hog!"

Jan ran her hand into his pants and now he was trapped. Breasts were attacking from the sides, hands were grabbing his cock, his balls, and squeezing mercilessly.

"Oh, fuck!" he whimpered, his legs weakening as Donna squeezed too hard.

Then Jan asked, "Which of us has the hardest buns, Tom?"

"What?" he squeaked.

They let go of him, laughing and giggling, and turned around and bent over.

"Best butt contest!" chirped Donna.
"Feel! Tell us who's best!"
"And you have to be honest! None of this tie stuff."
Tom stood, aware that he had to watch the steaks. Knowing that he was in very dangerous territory.
"Come on, grab ass, Tommy Boy!"
More giggles.
"I can't judge! I'm married so I'm biased."
"Oh, come on," begged Jan. "You can be honest this once. You know I won't get mad."
No. Not now. But as soon as Donna leaves my life will become a hell! So her ass is better than mine! You brute! You're sleeping in the guest room...no, the garage...no, in the doghouse!
"I'm not going to say."
"Well, at least feel us, please?"
"Pretty please?"
"Come on, feel our ass!"
And they began to chant, getting louder and louder, so loud that Tim was afraid the neighbors might hear.
"Feel our ass! Feel our ass! Feel our ass!"
"Okay," he caved. He put the spatula down, turned and grabbed a pair of delicious buns.
And they were delicious. As to whose was softer, he really couldn't judge. Donna's might be a little firmer, but Jan's had that familiar, sexy feel to it.
"Whose is better! Whose is better! Whose is—"
"This one!" he slapped both of them at the same time.
The girls laughed and each actually thought he had chosen them. They really were high.
They were now standing next to each other, facing him, and Jan arched her back and thrust her breasts forward.
"Feel my tits! Feel my tits!"
They were laughing hysterically, and the only way Tom could get them to stop was to reach out and feel their tits.
Large but perky. Stiff nipples. Soft sighs as he squeezed, then they moved into him and view to kiss him.
Their hands fought for his cock in his pants, their lips kissed his mouth, and they slowly pressed him back.
"OW!" He had bumped into the grill with his ass.

Tom lay on the lounge chair, his swim suit down and Jan and Donna, still chuckling, took turns with the salve.
"He really did burn the meat," whispered Donna.
"I like mine well done, anyway." More laughter.

"Hardee har," stated Tom.

Which cracked them up.

"Look," he said. "You girls are going to have to take it easy. You've got me outnumbered, and you're picking on me."

"Watch this," whispered Donna, and before Tom could do anything she rubbed his brown star.

"Hey!" He struggled, but the girls sat on him.

"Ow!"

"Oh, sorry," said Jan, moving off his burn mark.

It wasn't a bad burn, about as serious as a sunburn, and it would be gone by tomorrow. But right then it didn't feel too good.

"Not that! Get your finger out of my butt!"

But Donna stayed with it, and the girls were almost collapsing with laughter now.

"You've actually got him pinned down!"

"If he moves up it goes deeper. Isn't it fun, Tom?"

"No!" He sounded like he was gargling frogs.

She wiggled it briefly, then pulled it back. The girls just sat on either side of him then, sipping their martini's and getting ever drunker.

"Did you know men like to take it up the rear?"

"No! They don't!"

"You protesteth too much."

"Really?"

"Oh, yes. I've got a strap on in my luggage. You can borrow it if you want."

"Oh, that would be fun!"

"NO!" Tom wiggled and struggled and finally managed to dislodge Donna's finger and get up off the lounge.

"Come on, Tom. You'd love it." Then Donna leaned over to Jan and whispered, "He likes other stuff, too."

Jan blinked, "Like what?"

"Tom was frozen. His secret was coming out. Donna had said she wouldn't tell, but here she was, getting ready to blab!"

"Hey, there's no secret!"

"He was eating his own cum."

Jan looked up at Tom and her eyes widened.

"We surprised him when we came home yesterday, and he claimed he was hiding the evidence. But…I think he likes it. He probably does it all the time."

"Is that true, Tom?" Jan sat up and stared at him, and there was a very contemplative look in her eyes.

"No!" But from the guilty look on his face, she knew it.

"My husband is a cum eater."

"I am not! It just happened once, and it was an accident!"

"Man accidentally eats own cum? I think not!" Jan gave a laugh that was halfway between doubt and a snicker.

"I've been teasing him, hoping I could get him to eat his own cum for me, but you know men. They have all these little secrets…"

"I don't have any secrets!"

"Does, too," nodded Donna.

Tom had had enough. He started to leave.

"Hey! Finish cooking the steaks."

In spite of his mortification, he had to come back and take the steaks off the grill. He placed them on plates, and now that he was back, he allowed himself to sit down at the table as they ate.

And all night, while Tom retreated to his computer room, the girls whispered and connived.

Miserable, Tom worked, and he thought, *Things can't get much worse.*

But they could.

The next day his ass was pretty much feeling better, and the girls left him alone. They weren't drunk now, but they were still whispering, and he didn't like it. The way they kept glancing at him and grinning.

But it seemed like the initial storm had blown over, and if he could just get them to lighten up on the alcohol, maybe he could survive the next few weeks.

Then disaster hit.

Ding a ding ding! Jan's cell phone rang.

"Oh, it's work. Let me take this."

Tom was in his computer room, and he heard her talking right outside his window.

"Oh, my gosh! Is he okay? Oh, I understand. Sure, I can do that. I'll leave on a plane tonight."

Tom ran out to the patio and arrived just as Jan hung up the phone. "What's going on?"

"The store manager in Wichita had an accident. I need to go cover for him until they can get a replacement."

"Oh, no!"

"It's okay. He's okay." She thought he was saying 'oh, no' for the accident victim. In reality he was saying 'oh, no' because he knew that Jan was going to leave him with…Donna.

"Come on, I have to pack."

She led the way into the house, calling out, "Donna! Can you come here?"

In the bedroom Tom got out the suitcases and Jan threw clothes into the luggage.

"I can go back to the hotel."

"Nonsense. You'll stay right here."

Then the bomb dropped. "With the cum eater?"

Tom's mouth opened.

The girls giggled, both stood up and stared at him.

"Wait a minute."

"He is a horn dog."

"The way he latched onto our tits and buns last night…I don't think you can trust him."

"It's her! You can't trust Donna!"

"What should I do?"

"Didn't you say you had a chastity device?"

Jan brightened up and snapped her fingers. "Of course! The chastity tube!"

"No!" Tom wailed! "I hate that thing!"

"Hate has got nothing to do with it," stated Donna. "Trust does."

"But you can trust me! I would never make love to…to…"

"He says that now, but a couple of days without you to keep him in control…" Donna shrugged.

"Tom, go get the chastity device."

"No!"

"Donna, could you give us a moment?"

"Surely." She left the room.

Jan turned to Tom with a smile. "It's just for a week."

"I don't care! I shouldn't have to wear a chastity device in my own home!"

She stepped closer to him. "Honey?"

He should have heard the warning in her voice, but he was mounting such resistance he didn't catch it.

She grabbed his balls and squeezed. He fell to his knees and she hissed in his ear. "Listen, you stupid horn dog! I'm not going to risk my marriage just because you have no self discipline. Now you're going to put that chastity tube on. Now. Or I'll squeeze these puppies until they pop!

He had no choice. Tears seeped out of his eyes. He couldn't get ahold of her fingers to pry her off.

He nodded. "Okay."

She let go, stepped back, and waited.

He struggled to his feet, crossed to the dresser like a beaten dog, and got out the chastity tube.

She watched as he pulled off his pants and slipped it on his cock, put the ring over his whole package, and fastened them together.

He had been limp from the mangling she had just given him, but now his cock surged. There was just something about being put in prison that made a man struggle.

She smiled as he groaned.

"Donna!" she called out.

"Hey! Wait!"

Too late. Donna must have been waiting right outside, and she burst in and looked straight at him. "Oh, yes," she licked her lips.

Jan grabbed Tom by the chastity tube and walked across the room, pulled him down the hallway to the kitchen.

"Hey! Come on! I've got it on."

"Yep, and it's going to stay on."

She opened the catch all drawer and took out a tube of glue.

"And this is going to make sure!" She squeezed glue into the hole of the little padlock.

"I know that you have another key somewhere, but this will make sure you don't use it. You can cut it off when I get home. Until then…" she held the lock while it dried and grinned up at him.

"Oh, my gosh!" Donna was caught between a laugh and a snicker. "This is too good to be true!"

Still holding the little lock, Jan stated in hard tones, "Now you kids can play. Do whatever you want. You can even sleep together. But…no fuckee fuck. You got that?"

His cock was going hog wild in the tube. It was flattened out against the insides, surging, and he could feel the terrible sense of deprivation and lust coming over him.

Then Jan turned to Donna. "In fact, maybe you can break him in. You know, that pegging thing you were telling me about. You said you had a strap on?"

"Oh, I do." Donna couldn't take her eyes off Tom. She was staring at him like a one-eyed cat in a fish store.

Then Jan turned to Tom. "You hear that? You do everything Donna asks. No questions. Absolute obedience. You got that."

Tom didn't answer.

"Excellent. Now that that's all taken care of…I'm going to finish my packing."

Part Two

Tom took Jan to the airport. It was an hour away and he was unreasonably surly during the drive.

"What are you complaining about?" asked Jan. "It's only a week, and just think how much you're going to love it when I get back. Why, we'll make love all day long, and you'll have the best squirt of your life!"

"But I don't want to be locked up!"

"You've enjoyed our little games before."

"Yeah, but that was when it was you and me."

"Oh, so that's it. You're scared of Donna."

He didn't want to admit it, but silence is a reasonable confession.

"Heck, she'll just tease you a little."

"What's this about breaking me in?"

"That? Oh, that's just a joke thing. We were talking about that yesterday, and…it's nothing."

He mumbled something.

"What?"

"It's no joke when my sex is concerned."

"You're just being overly sensitive. Now, man up and enjoy yourself."

"But what's this business about me doing everything she says?"

"I know you have a little problem with Donna, but if you do everything she says then she can't complain, and you might even find that you like her."

He mumbled something else, but Jan didn't bother asking him what.

Tom opened the door and stepped into the house.

It felt different. His wife hadn't been gone but an hour or so and…it was different.

A different feel.

A different ambience, a smell, an atmosphere.

"Oh, fuck," he muttered to himself, then he headed for the office.

Donna was already in his office. She had his computer powered up and she was looking at…porn!

"Hey!"

"Hey is for horses and cows that go moo. Look at this!"

She had the screen open to IXXX. The category had to do with 'male submissives.' The movie showed a fellow on a bed, on his back, his legs pressed up around his ears and a woman doing him Amazon.

"Now that is the way to do sex."

Tom stared at the images. He was fascinated by the way the woman kept pumping the man like she was the man and he was the woman.

"Don't you wish you could do this?"

He said nothing. His cock revolted in his cage.

"I wish I could do this." She contemplated him with slightly closed eyes. "Man, I'd love to bend you over and..." she turned back to the screen and pulled up another image.

A man on a bed, upside down against the wall at the head of the bed. A woman was pushing a dildo in his ass and stroking him, and suddenly the man squirted.

It was a big spurt of cream and it went right into his mouth.

Tom was caught. He didn't want to watch, but he couldn't get away.

He had caught semen with his hand and literally threw it into his mouth. but this...this was right from the course.

"Whoa! Look at that fool gobble!" Donna chuckled, made the image whole screen, and they cold see big spurts and drops going into the man's mouth.

Finally, Tom turned around.

"Wait a minute," she caught his sleeve, "where are you going?"

He stood, breathing, his shoulders slumped. In an odd way he knew what was coming. And while he was frightened, there was an excitement boiling within.

She pulled him around, stood him in front of her and she undid his buckles, then his zipper. She pulled his pants down and there is was. A two inch tube full of limp cock.

Limp cock that was trying hard not to be limp.

She held his balls and smiled up at him. "Tommy Boy. No more clothes. Not while I'm in charge."

She held him, rose up, kissed him, then she began undressing him all the way.

He thought about fighting, but how do you fight a woman? Especially when she's holding your balls?

She divested him of clothing, made him totally nude, then she took off her dress. She didn't get undressed all the way. She knew that a woman in lingerie actually has more appeal than a totally naked woman.

She kissed him. She grabbed his buns and held him to her.

He felt her big breasts pressing against his chest. He felt his cock wiggling like crazy down there, and unable to do anything.

She laughed and slithered down. She kissed his nipples, sucked his balls, then slithered up.

"We're going to have fun," she whispered.

"No!" he moaned.

"Do you remember the part where you're supposed to do anything I say?"

"No."

She laughed, then took his hand and dragged him out to the kitchen.

"This next part is always the tough part. At least when it begins. Once you're broken in it'll be fun."

"Broken in? Like with…with that pegging thing?"

"Oh, no!" she smirked. "Not yet. That comes later. First you have to look like you deserve it. Now, get down the bourbon. Let's have a drink and just enjoy the moment."

"I don't want to drink."

"Honey, when I start working on you…you're going to want a drink. Now, it's up there," she pointed at the liquor cabinet.

Tom saw the truth of this, and he needed a drink. He got down an amber bottle while Donna filled two glasses with ice.

He poured in the bourbon and she followed it up with a bit of Coke.

He sipped, and stood there while she sipped, inches from him, smiling at him, feeling his balls.

"Why are you doing this?" he asked, half a glass down.

"Because I can." She kissed him, deeply. While she kissed him she put her glass down and reached around and held his buttocks.

"God! What a hammer!"

"But…it doesn't do you any good! You can't cum either!"

"Of course I can. Fingers and fists, dildos and vibrators. And so can you."

"No, I can't. I'm locked up."

"That doesn't matter. I can get the sperm out of you in two minutes."

"Prove it."

It spurted out of him, a challenge, because he was already feeling the heat.

"Naw! You have to be deserving. You have to look like you want it. Here, I'll make us another one."

She made his drink stiff, and hers…unstiff. He drank 3/4s bourbon and she drank 3/4s Coke.

And he had no clue. He was just desperate, befuddled, and trying to survive.

And another drink.

Now he was feeling pretty loose. His inhibitions were evaporating like yesterday's rain and he was feeling no pain. Nor resentment nor fear.

They were now in the living room, him naked and sucking down the booze, and her semi-naked and sipping delicately.

She was waiting, and when he started kissing her, in spite of the fact that he had no dick in service, she knew he was ready.

"Come on, honey. It's time to get you ready."

"Ready for what?" he asked, as she led him by the cock down the hall.

"Ready for anything. Ready to make you deserving. Ready to have fun."

She took him into his bedroom and pushed him over the bed. "Stay there."

He stayed, giggling, and she opened her suitcase—it had been moved into the master bedroom—and took out a butt plug.

She greased it up and slid it right into him.

"Whoa!" But he was so drunk he just accepted it. Didn't get all rigid or anything.

"Nice fit, Mr. Tight Ass."

"I ain't not no tight ass!" he chortled.

"Now now," she agreed. "Now, I need to get rid of your hair."

He felt the top of his head. "But it took me a long time to grow this!"

He had a healthy mop, long enough to be styled, but usually kept masculine.

"Not that hair." She pushed him into the bathroom and produced a bottle of Nair.

He stood there while she slathered it all over him. She got under his arms, over his back, down his legs. He giggled when she spent a long time making sure the stuff was really smushed into his groin.

"You're a hair thief," he laughed.

"I am, she said, and while they waited she kissed him, again and again and again, and laughed at the way his worm wiggled in its cage.

"God, you poor man," she sympathized with a laugh.

Then she put him in the shower and told him to rinse off.

He rinsed.

She handed him an expensive shampoo.

He 'shamped,' as he called it.

Then the conditioner.

When he was done she got him out, dried him off, and began styling his hair. She brushed it into a feminine flip, and was delighted with how long it was.

Then, lest he sober up, she got him another drink.

He sat at his wife's vanity table and Donna painted his face. She took her time, kissing him occasionally, hefting his chastity cage every once in a while, and put on primer and foundation, blush and all the other wonderful smelling chemicals that make a woman beautiful.

He stared at himself, felt his skin, and marveled.

"Wow."

"You ain't seen nothing, yet, Tommy Boy."

She lengthened and curled his eyelashes, shadowed his eyes, and applied lipstick.

He stared at himself in the mirror. A woman, be it with a cock in chastity and no tits.

"I don't have any boobies! he cried.

"Don't wet your face," she admonished. "We'll handle that."

To give him breasts she put a piece of tape on his pectorals and pulled them towards each other. She put a bra on him. It was tight, and between the tape and the bra his chest was pushed together and he actually had cleavage.

"Wow."

All the time she had been taking pictures with her cell, and now she focused on his cleavage. Then she frowned and applied some make up, darkened some areas, lightened others, and, trick of the lighting and make up, it looked like he had a serious canyon.

"Fuck!" he whispered. "I really have a pair."

"You do. Now, hold on."

He stood very still and she took a small pair of. scissors and cut holes for his nipples to poke through.

His nipples, courtesy of his horniness, were extremely erect, and the cup material was very smooth, and when she pulled a tight dress over his head it looked like he wasn't wearing much of a bra. He had cleavage, and his nipples popped out, and…he actually looked feminine.

Donna took a small string and tied his chastity cage between his legs, looping the string up and tying it to the back of his garter belt.

He was set. A sexy looking woman.

Donna took more pictures of him, then fixed yet another drink.

Tom walked around the house in high heels, listening to the sound of his heels clicking. Looking down at his faux cleavage. Admiring his reflection in mirrors and on windows.

Wow! he thought.

"Well, Tom, how's your butt?"

He felt his butt and sighed. He had been aware of it all morning. He felt it when he sat down, he felt it when he walked. It was such a wonderful, warm feeling.

"Do you like it?"

"Oh, yeah!"

She was holding the phone loosely, recording on video.

"And did you like eating your own cum?"

"That was fun! And it tasted so good."

He knew, somewhere in his dazed, addled, drunken mind, that he shouldn't be saying such things, but…he felt so good!

What's the harm in admitting to a little kink, eh?

"That's great, Tom. Say, let's go for a drive!"

"A drive?" he frowned, something was wrong.

Donna took his arm and gave him another drink and walked him out to the car.

He smiled at the sight of his blue Malibu. It was a classic car.

"I'll put the top down," Donna said, and she got behind the wheel.

A minute later they were cruising through town, two beautiful women enjoying the wind in their hair.

Tom loved it. He held his glass low so nobody could see it, and he waved to people, and people waved back. Especially the young and virile male type of people.

Then they pulled into a hamburger stand, one of the old kind with carhops.

They ordered burgers and fries and Cokes…and Donna added some booze to the Cokes when they arrived, and shortly they had a half a dozen studly, young men crowded around the car.

This surprised Tom, but he was too drunk.

The young men knew it, and they flirted, and wished they could climb in. Then Donna asked them a question. Her phone recording, she asked, "Hey, guys, which of you would like to get a blow job?"

They all grinned and raised their hands.

"And which of you would like to get a blow job from my cum loving friend here?"

Tom was out of it. He grinned at the cell phone as all the young men, bulges in their pants, raised their hands.

"And how many of you would like to put your big, fat penises into her vagina?"

All the hands shot up. Some of them shot two hands up. They were all wondering if they were really going to get lucky!

Then Donna asked her last question. "And how many of you would like to fuck her if you knew that she wasn't a woman, but a man?"

Faces froze. Young men stepped back. Suddenly they all disappeared.

"Well," said Donna, focusing on Tom's face. "Sorry, Tom. But you'll have to get your jollies elsewhere."

"Oh, darn?" he blubbered, not sure what he was talking about.

They went back to Tom's house and Donna gave him his last drink of the night. It was more Coke than bourbon because he was just about done for.

She led him into his room and dug through her luggage. She brought out a large dildo with big balls. The thing was a very special penis, with hollow balls and a tube running to the slit in the head.

She filled the balls with a white concoction of milk thickened with sugar.

"Tommy?"

"Yeah?" He looked around blearily.

"I need you to do a little fuck and suck."

He grinned. He had forgotten that his dick was in chastity.

"No, honey. You're going to suck me off, and I'm going to fuck you."

"What?" He was surprised, but not unduly protesting. He was that drunk.

"Now lay down here, and let me set up the phone there..." She arranged the phone so it would only show his butt and the penis.

She then put the dildo to his butt and began gently screwing him.

"Oh, yeah!" he howled. "I like it!"

Hell, he wouldn't even remember it. But whether he was actually enjoying it or not, he would learn to enjoy it in the future.

Donna arranged the phone and his position several times, making it look like he was getting screwed by a man, but never revealing the body of the man. It took some doing, but with improper lighting it was going to work.

Finally, she had enough footage, and she took the dildo out.

Tom was really gone now. She had to slap him a bit to make him function, but she managed to get him on his knees. She arranged the phone so it would show penis, but not the back of it, not that it was a strap on.

Then she pumped his mouth, squeezed the balls, and white semen looking fluid bulged out of his mouth.

"Fuck!" Tom blurted, choking a little, and then, a perfect punctuation mark, he threw up.

"BLAH!" and the cell phone caught it all.

Donna spent an hour loading the video to his computer, editing it, and then uploading it to her own cloud account.

Finally, she was done.

She grinned, took off her clothes, and jumped into bed and snuggled against Tom.

Mmm. Men. They were so much fun.

The sun splattered against the wall, crept down over the headboard, then into the eyes of the sleeping Tom.

"Unh...uh..." He spluttered, then opened his eyes.

They were filled with red, squiggly lines. Looked like a darned road map.

He felt the arm across his chest, his taped and sexy, bulging chest, and smiled. Then he panicked.

Jan had come home early! She would find him in a bra having tits, and—he fell out of the bed.

Donna blinked a few times and looked at him, then she began to laugh.

He looked so silly sitting on the floor, his make up a little smeared, in his lingerie.

"What…what are you doing?"

"I was sleeping. What are you doing?"

"I…we…we didn't fuck did we?"

She laughed and said, "Look at your ding dong."

He looked down, saw the comfort and discomfort of his worm, wiggling frantically in his cage.

Oh, that was what had woken him up, the pain of a morning woody.

He scrambled to his feet, almost fell down, and headed for the bathroom.

"Oh, heysoos! Heysoos!" he muttered. He remembered he had to sit to pee, and sat on the throne and spritzed the water below.

"Oh, fuck!" he sighed in relief. Then he looked through the door to where Donna was laying on the bed and laughing.

"What did…why are you in here?"

She shook her head sadly. "You don't remember what you did last night?"

"What I did?" His head was starting to bang now, and it felt like the world was sliding sideways.

"Sure. You had a lot of fun last night. Want to see?"

"Do I want…"

She laughed. "You're still a little drunk. But come on, I'll show you.

She got out of bed, naked, and waited for him to stop tinkling.

She took him into the computer room, sat him down, got him a bloody Mary for the pain, and powered up the computer.

He sat and sipped and watched, and his jaw slowly dropped open, and the pain in his head was replaced by shock and awe.

Him, in drag, laughing and his hair flowing in the breeze of the moving car. Well, not drag, he was actually fixed up pretty good. He looked like a real woman. They pulled into the carhop place on the other side of town.

Cut to young men with muscles in their tight tee shirts. The camera picking up flirtatious banter, and occasionally focusing on the bulges in the men's pants.

Cut to questions.

Like a blow job? Hands up. Tom grinning.

Put their penises in her vagina? Hands up. Tom grinning.

Then: "And how many of you would like to fuck her if you knew that she wasn't a woman, but a man?"

A clever bit of editing, all hands went up!

And Tom grinned.

Cut to the house, Tom getting buggered, and loving it.

Tom sucking a cock, and the cock spurting.

Tom throwing up all over the cock.

Finis. No titles.

"No!" he whispered through the shock.

"Well, not really. All of that happened, but I have to admit it took a bit of editing to create that wonderful production."

"But…why? Why are you doing this?"

But she was intent on explaining her role as a director and editor. "I had to get tricky, and I did put a dildo in your ass. But, those shots are real. Tommy Boy, you really did love it when I showed you how the other half lives. And that blow job, that was perfect. You did it all, then threw up. God! That was amazing! I couldn't have planned that!"

"But why? Why did you do this?"

Donna stopped the computer. On the monitor he was frozen with a mouthful of exploding cock. She turned to him.

"Tommy, honey. You're a man." As if that explained everything.

"But…but…"

She held up her hand. "It was all a plan. Jan and I didn't just run into each other. We planned this out. I came to town, I had all the toys I needed, as did she. And there wasn't any emergency. She didn't get on the plane. She had a Starbuck's, waited for you to clear the parking lot, then went to a hotel and checked in.

"To be honest, we thought this would take a while. We figured it would take the full three weeks, and maybe even more, to set you up. But you went in less than two days. In a short while I'll give Jan a call and you can go pick her up."

"But…but…I still don't understand why!"

"Because men need to be broken in. They need to be trained. Oh, she could have done it the long way, taken a year to break you down, get you used to the proper order of things, but she's an impatient girl, is our Jan, and she asked me to help her get this done the fast way."

Now Tom was silent, his mind trying to grasp the significance of it all.

"Tom. You're going to live as a woman now, and Donna has decided that she would rather be the one wielding the penis. You're going to be the one bending over and taking it, and that's the way it should be."

"It should?" His face showed a curious lack of expression. He was actually going into shock.

"You'll be in chastity from now on, and you'll be called upon to wear a strap on when needed, and you'll get to do cunnilingus daily. A lot of it. But you won't be on the giving end any more. Women are taking over, and you're going to be on the receiving end. Believe me, it will be wonderful. You'll get to do the housework, and you'll wait on Jan hand

and foot. And me! I'll be around a lot more. Jan prefers to make love to women, and I'm all right with that."

Tom gulped, made a sobbing sound, and gasped.

"There, there, it's all right. Now, let's get you fixed up. Jan is going to want you as a woman when you pick her up."

Helpless, totally outgunned, Tom followed Donna back to the bedroom. His cock cried pre-cum in its cage, and his chest heaved every once in a while in a sob.

But there was in his chest a little piece of relief. And that relief would grow with time until he came to grips with the new world order, and his place in the scheme of things.

At the vanity table Donna sat him down and, with a large smile, painted his lips bright red.

END

The Jamaican Sex Change!

A couple swap sexes,
male to female and female to male!

Grace Mansfield

A Note from the Author!

Walk a mile in their shoes. But it goes for both sexes. Maybe then men would understand women, and women, well, we already understand men.

But, would you be a man for a day if it made your man into a woman for a day?

Or a week or a month?

Try a trip down to Jamaica, find out what those wicked, old witch doctors have been hiding from the rest of the world.

You'll be glad you did!

STAY HORNY!

Gracie

Part One

"Let's go to Jamaica!" Lyn said.

"Why on earth wold anybody want to go to Jamaica?" Dave asked.

They were at a restaurant in Santa Monica. Charley Coyote. A nightclub by night, it served up the best ribs in All of Southern California.

Lyn was looking good. Her hair was dirty blonde, shiny, up in the French style. Her light blue eyes were opaque to look at, but looked right through whoever looked at them. Her body...whoa!

Dave was a slender fellow. He ate one meal a day, practiced yoga for three hours a day, and had a peaceful manner on his sturdy face.

Lyn chewed delicately on a rib, nibbling at the sauce and the charred flesh gently. She paused, then, "Because it's the land of magic."

"Yeah," he scoffed. "Black magic!"

"So you're afraid you're going to get cursed?" she teased.

"I've already been cursed," he muttered as he sampled the mashed potatoes.

"Huh?"

"Yeah, you know. My penis. It's too big." He looked so sad and she giggled.

"It's so never ending, you mean."

"Well, that, too. But I don't have much interest in Jamaica. I'd probably run into a Houngan and he curse me with a limp dick."

"Houngan? What do you know about Houngans?"

"Vodoun witch doctors. Medicine, healing, and...black magic."

"That's only if you piss them off."

"I don't intend to be anywhere near them, so much for pissing them off."

She frowned, her mouth a little twisted. She had a three month vacation coming up and she wanted to do a little traveling.

"Besides. They have hurricanes there."

"And you're afraid of a little wind."

He grinned. A 200 mile per hour blow job. Yep."

"Well, listen. I think you're wrong, and I'll prove it."

"You will, eh?"

"Yep. I'm going to curse you right now. My own special spell."

"You know, all joking aside, I don't really like to joke about curses."

"Scared?"

"Respectful. There's a lot of things in this world that we don't understand. I'd prefer to be on the good side of everything."

"Oh, pooh. You're no fun."

"I'll drink to that."

But Lyn recovered her good humor in a split second. "So this curse?"

He groaned and rolled his eyes upward.

"You're not going to get off until you go to Jamaica."

"What?"

"You heard me. You won't be able to cum until you go to Jamaica."

"That's the stupidest curse I ever heard."

She smiled. "Yep."

She made some wavy motions in the air with her fingers, said "Booga booga. Now you're cursed."

The odd thing was that right as she said that, at the very moment of 'cursing' him, he felt a small pain in his groin. It was sort of above his pecker, in the soft area below his abdomen, and it was a sharp twinge.

"Ah, fuck," he whispered, putting a rib bone down on the plate.

"What?"

"I just got a pain down in the pubic area."

She gloated, "See? I really know how to throw a curse."

"Poppy cock."

"Cock? Did you say cock?" she laughed.

He took a sip of his tea and took a deep breath. The sharp pain lessened, but it was still there. That was so odd. It felt like he had torn a muscle, or had a hernia.

But he was lithe, very stretched out, courtesy of all the yoga he did. He knew he didn't have a physical ailment. So what the heck?

They finished lunch, he paid, and they headed for his apartment.

They lived in a second floor apartment above Hollywood Ave. The west part of Hollywood Ave which had apartments lining the sides of the streets. Runyon Park was right around the corner.

All the way home Dave had a pain below his gut, above his groin. It waned, then grew a little, then waned again, but by the time he was walking up his stairs it almost had him doubled over.

"Are you all right?" asked Lyn. "I didn't mean to curse you."

"It's all right. I just want to lie down."

He lay on the couch and Lyn sat on the balcony and read a Grace Mansfield novel.

She liked Grace. Loony plots and real-ish characters. And the sex… woo woo!

By the time dinner rolled around Dave was feeling better. He skipped dinner, he had already used up his one meal a day on lunch. Besides, his belly didn't hurt, it sort of churned.

They watched a little TV, then got ready for bed.

He got ready for bed.

She got ready for sex.

"Oh honey," he groaned. "I don't feel all that good."

"But that wasn't a real curse!"

"You don't know your own power."

So they slept, and he felt the same the next day, a little off, a little pain that came and went. He felt so off he skipped his yoga class and just slept.

Then it was Sunday, and he was fine. The extra rest seemed to have done it.

Lyn sighed in relief and teased him all day. But, weird, he wasn't responsive. He got a little chub, but none of that king sized boner stuff he usually did.

After dinner they went to bed and she rolled over on him, pinned him, kissed him, and stopped. "What's wrong?"

"I'm not getting hard."

"I know that. I can feel it. What's wrong? is it me?"

"I don't know. It's not you, but…I think it's that thing I had yesterday."

"But I thought that was just a flu or something."

"So did I. But I'm thinking different now."

So they slept without screwing. Very frustrating, but sometimes it happens. Though it had never happened to them. To him. He was so damned healthy from all the yoga that he was ALWAYS able to get it up.

In the morning, his penis still unresponsive, he decided to see a doctor.

"I felt a sharp pain here," he pointed to a spot midway between his penis and his belly button. "It lasted for a while, got pretty bad, then it went away."

"But you haven't had an erection since then?" The doctor was a young lady, oriental, long black hair and unusually large breasts for an oriental. Her almond eyes considered him, and she lifted her stethoscope.

"Breath."

He breathed, and she listened, and tapped, and took his blood pressure, then even asked for a blood sample.

Finally, she was done with the general part, and she asked to see his penis.

"Uh…" he turned a little red, but he stood and unzipped.

He reached in and pulled out his limp weenie and she held it in her hand.

She palpated it, and that alone should have made it pulse and throb.

It lay like a comatose slug in her hand.

She felt it, pressing her fingers into the shaft at various points.

He felt it, and it felt good, but she couldn't get a rise out of him.

She held his testicles and felt them.

"Fuck," he whispered under his breath. This felt good! Why wasn't anything happening?

She let go and smiled at him.

He tucked himself in and she turned to her desk and wrote her notes.

"It might be an infection, but I won't be sure until we've got the lab work back."

"So I should just go home and...go home?" He sounded a bit miserable and she looked up, then gave a wan smile.

"Dave, it might just be stress, or tiredness. Or it might be for no discernible reason. But that's erectile dysfunction for you. I'll look at the lab results and let you know in the next couple of days. Until then, just take it easy. No hard exercise, no stress, don't drink or smoke. Okay."

"What about teaching yoga? I usually do a lot of that."

She shook her head, her dark eyes showing a glint. "No. Nothing but rest. If it is just stress, then you should probably just take a vacation. Go to the Bahamas or something."

Dave was reminded of Lyn's desire to go to Jamaica.

"Well, all right. What about dope? Can you give me a prescription for some really good drugs? Maybe a key of H?"

She laughed. "Sure, green tea and yogurt."

"Party pooper."

They laughed and he left.

He hung out that day, and it was difficult.

Lyn was a school teacher and was off for the summer, and she was, after a year of handling brats, horny and lustful and filled with desire.

And he was limp and discouraged.

"Heysoos," she muttered. "Can you at least pimp me out or something?"

That made him grin. "Just be patient, sweet cakes. I'm just between filling stations. A couple of days, a gallon of whiskey, and I'll be all over you."

"But you hardly ever drink!"

"If I'm limp I'll start," he quipped wryly.

So they stayed home, played Parcheesi, and waited for the doctor's call.

And she did try various things just to make sure he wasn't faking, that he really wasn't limp, but it just wasn't' happening.

The next day. He owned his own yoga studio so he had instructors to fill in for him, but he was sinking lower and lower.

"Jeez, this is frustrating," he whined.

"Imagine how I feel?" Lyn responded dourly.

The next day the doctor called.

"Dave, there's nothing wrong with you. Nothing that I can see."

"So it's what? Stress? Overwork? I work a lot, but it's mostly yoga, and I don't stress at all at that."

Then the doctor said a most interesting and unexpected thing. "Well, unless somebody cursed you, you just need to take a vacation. Take a long ocean voyage or something."

Dave blinked. A curse? Yesterday she talks about the Bahamas, and today she talks about a long ocean voyage, and Lyn wants to go to Jamaica. WTF?

Hanging up the phone he turned to Lyn and just stared at her.

"What?"

"This is your fault."

"Huh? What?"

"You cursed me."

"I…what? That was just a joke!"

"Joke or not, it worked. Doctor's orders, go to Jamaica and dance with sexy girls and drink lots of brown liquor."

"What! You mean it?" She was on her feet so fast her boobs bounced.

He shrugged. "Might as well. Lot's of rest, doesn't want me to do heavy physical activity. And I haven't had more than an occasional glass of wine for over ten years. Maybe it's time to take a break, cut loose, and have a good time. Can you make reservations?"

"Can I? Hoo, boy! Get out your credit card 'cause we're leaving tomorrow!"

He sang from the old John Denver song:

We're leaving on a jet plane,
don't know when we'll be back again…

Then Lyn was singing with him, holding his hands and jumping around and kissing him good and solid on the mouth.

But his penis just hung there.

They took a plane to Dallas, from there they flew five hours to cover the 1500 miles to Kingston.

They had flown before, and they enjoyed flying, meeting passengers, looking out the porthole from higher than a volcano spits. They talked and learned things, and even gave a little of their information to help others.

Unfortunately, Dave was in a light funk.

Who wouldn't be with their cock in a sling?

"It's okay, honey. Just relax. We'll have a drink and take it easy and before you know it, Weeee!" Just raised a single finger and waggled it.

He had to chuckle. "I know, it's just…well, you know."

"I know. Right now you feel like you're less than a man. You feel like you're a eunuch, that you have no use to the world, that your life is over, that—"

"Okay!" he blurted.

Lyn laughed, and he got it and laughed, too.

"Hey, it's only a dick, right?"

"Only a dick," he nodded, feeling like his life had ended.

It was a smooth landing and they stepped out into tropical heat.

"Woo!"

"Lucky it's not a hurricane," grinned a passenger next to them.

They stopped briefly at a bar, then headed for a hotel near the beach, and stopped for a drink downstairs, then went up to their room and had a drink from the minibar, and Dave was feeling pretty good. He rarely drank and he was already feeling a bit sloshy.

Lyn was actually better at holding her liquor, and she had to laugh at the way he was acting, uncoordinated, confused, happy.

"See! I told you. It's only a dick!"

"Yee haw! Only a dick! I'll take another drink."

"Let's get to the beach, then we can drink down there."

"Okay. Where's my suit. Here's my suit. I'll put on my suit."

But he grabbed the bottom of her two piece by mistake, didn't realize it because the color was the same as his, and stepped into them. He pulled them up and stepped in a weird circle trying to figure out what was wrong.

"What the fuck?"

Lyn saw what was happening, and decided to joke with him. "You don't have it on right."

"Oh. But…it's only a dick." And laughed.

She went to him, gently slid her bottoms around on him, reached in and pushed his limp dick down between his legs, and pulled the bottoms up snug.

He looked ridiculous. And…sort of sexy.

They were tighter and better than Speedos. Or worse.

She thought better. She looked at his smooth front and…it was sort of cool. It was sexy. No dick, just a smooth front. And it was a good thing he kept himself shaved down there, because hair would have sprouted like a well watered garden.

And he didn't realize that he was wearing her bottoms.

"How do I look?" he asked, his grin cock-eyed, his eyes a little unsteady.

"Beautiful, honey. Let me get my suit on."

She had packed two bathing suits, and she quickly stripped and dressed.

Her other suit was a bit risqué, and she bulged over the top. But it was worth it to see his bottom looking so…feminine. And she wondered what he would look like if he put on the top.

He didn't have any tits, but just the effect, the visual of him looking so sweet and cute. She could comb his long hair into a style, and she could, put lip…she shook herself, ended her fantasies, and grabbed him by the hand.

"Come on, honey, before the water melts."

"Water melts? I…how does water…melt?"

She laughed and they picked up towels and stepped into the hallway.

At that moment a large, black man in a bell hop suit two sizes too small—his cock looked like a giant banana outlined in his tight, little monkey suit—passed by. He was pushing a cart with a suit hanging on it and several matched suitcases on the bottom, and he took one look at Dave and grinned. "Batty boy. You here for obeah." He stopped and took out a business card. He was apparently the go to boy in the hotel because he had a pocket full of the small cards. He scribbled on back. "You call here. Best Obeah in Jamaica." He pushed the card into Dave's hand, then pushed the cart down the hall..

Dave stared stupidly at the 3 1/2 by 2 card.

Lyn took it out of his hands and slipped it under their door. "We'll look at it when we get back."

"Okay!"

Hand in hand, their bottoms looking smooth and sexy, they headed towards the elevator.

Dave got a few snickers when he crossed the lobby, and one lady pointed rudely, but they were on vacation, as were other people, and it was more of a live and let live atmosphere.

A couple of the islanders frowned, then masked their frowns. If white wanted to have pum pum, play transgenda, that okay. Long as they spend money and tip good.

Out onto the beach, and the sand was white and smooth. They slid their feet through the minuscule grains like they were ice skating.

Stopped at a little bar and bought some drinks. And headed out towards the waves.

By now Dave was pretty well out of it. Lyn laid a large towel on the sand and he lay down on his front.

Lyn, a bit of the pixie in her, said, "Lay on your back. You're looking a little too white on the front.

Dave, drunk, obliged.

Shortly he was snoring.

So she reached into her bag and took out a big scarf. She gave it a twisted in the center and arranged it on his chest so it looked like a bra.

Dave slept for an hour, unaware that his skin was turning red, and that he was going to have a white bra on his chest.

Finally, he awoke, looked around blearily, and stood up.

People around them chuckled, and a small child stared at him like something was wrong.

He stumbled down to the water and waded through the waves, then flopped down and floated.

Lyn went with him and they floated, and she kept her laughter in, and…they were on vacation!

"What the fuck?" Dave stared at himself in the mirror. His skin was red, and it looked like he had been wearing a bikini.

By now he had realized his mistake in the trunks, the bottom, but his chest!

"What happened? Why did you…"

What had Lyn done?

Lyn skated through his suspicions, "I threw a scarf on you to protect you from the sun. The wind must have shifted it on your chest.

He glared at her, but…she put a drink in his hand.

And she thought, *If I could keep him drunk I could probably change his sex!*

It was a funny thought, made her snicker, but she didn't rally intend to do something like that.

She picked up the card the bellhop had given Dave.

Batty Boy. Obeah. Jamaican terms, obviously. She typed Obeah into her translator.

The Act makes it illegal to be a 'person practicing Obeah', which it defines as: 'any person who, to effect any fraudulent or unlawful purpose, or for gain, or for the purpose of frightening any person, uses, or pretends to use any occult means, or pretends to possess any supernatural power or knowledge.

Whoa! Supernatural power! One day and they were already finding out about 'black magic.'

She tapped the card against her front teeth.

Black magic. What was the difference between black magic and white magic? One used for good, one for bad. But all they wanted was for Dave to recover the use of his pecker. So…what if a witch doctor could actually do something? What if this 'Obeah' could give him a potion that was better than any viagra?

That left 'Batty boy,' but she didn't care about that. It probably just meant a man who had a bat for a cock, and the bellhop was using it facetiously, Dave not having a cock at all.

Dave was out on the patio. The sun was sliding down over the horizon and he was sipping his drink.

Obeah. Could an Obeah cure him?

She picked up her phone and dialed the number on the back.

"Hail. Whachoo wan?"

Thick accent, but friendly enough.

"I was given a card. My husband would like to...to..." Like to what? She thought, then said, "Do you give consultations?"

"Mi consult gud. You come come. Me consult. Ten dollah."

The lady on the other end gave an address and hung up. Just like that. No waiting on the phone while a robot says this call may be monitored for training purposes.

She sat for a moment, then made up her mind. "Dave! Get some clothes on! We're going places!"

The taxi was a 1956 Chevy with multi colored panels and fenders. The chrome was shiny, though, and it could actually do 25 miles an hour without shimmying too badly.

The driver was a scrawny black, very dark skin, midnight with no moon skin, and big, white teeth.

"You go Mama Bouchette. Boo Boo, she called. You say Madam. She be fine fine."

With such cheerful patter the driver took them to Tivoli Gardens, which was a little nerve wracking in itself. Tivoli was the equivalent of Detroit Projects, as evidenced by the surly young men smoking big MJ stogies and tapping their shoes to the sound of reggae. Bob Marley was timeless.

But the driver herded them right up to the Mama Bouchette's door, warning the thugs back with the dire phrase.

"We go Boo Boo. You no mess."

And they didn't mess. In a short half minute the driver pounded on a door, a door festooned with feathers and shells and little stick dolls and a rubber shrunken head, then simply opened the door. "You go in. She here."

Then the driver was gone, the door was closed, and Dave and Lyn looked at their surroundings.

Shabby couch, shabby chair, spring sprung.

Picture of Jesus in velvet on the wall, looking very neon under a bright light directed down on his visage.

A wall of books. Everything from Lee Childs to The Feminine Mystique.

Two lamps with shades that looked like they had been made in Nazi Germany, from human skin, complete with tattoos. A dull, yellow glow from each lamp lighting the room.

A rug worn through in places.

A mix of odors unbelievable. Everything from bath soap to incense to cooked chicken to vomit. A nasal melange of unprecedented proportion.

On the other side of the room was a door to the kitchen. The light coming from their was brighter than that of the two lamps.

"Back here! You come back here!"

Dave and Lyn walked gingerly back to the kitchen, staring about them every step of the way.

A woman was stirring a pot of something on an old gas stove. The stove was missing the little grills and the pot was suspended by a string from the ceiling.

"Um…yeah," the woman licked her finger in a taste test.

She was tall and skinny. No boobs to speak of. A dress that hung like a muu muu and was made of the brightest colors imaginable. Her hair was done up in dreadlocks and she had thick eye make up on.

Dark eyes, dark skin, dark eye liner…her eyes looked like caves with but a far away glimmer of light in them.

"You want chicken soup? Good for soul." She cackled.

She had a flat nose, thick lips and a tattoo of Jesus right square on her forehead.

"Uh, no. I called about a consultation."

"How bout you, Batty Boy? You want soup? Good for what ails you."

She spoke the right words, but mangled them with her accent. Still, she was very understandable.

"Uh, no thanks."

She looked at him under the rim of her granny glasses. "No thank. You polite. Hah!" She turned back to the stove and stirred some more.

"Uh, you said you had consultations?"

"Oh, yeah. Me talk talk. Fix you up good." She looked at them again, again holding up her little spectacles. "If you be fix fix. What wrong? No bloody month?"

"No! It's Dave here. My husband."

"What wrong with Batty Boy. He look okay."

"His, uh, his sex doesn't work."

Mama Boo Boo put the spoon down, turned and inspected Dave.

Dave felt very awkward.

She shuffled across the kitchen and grabbed his groin.

"Urk!"

Lyn blinked and her mouth opened.

Mama Boo Boo felt his manhood roughly. Jerked it up and down, then let go.

"Him messed bad. You curse good. Penis dick stay limp long time." She went back to her hanging pot.

"But I didn't curse him. I mean, I did, but I didn't…it's really a curse?"

"Oh, it good curse. You strong woman. You stay here I teach. We make zombie together." She cackled, then tasted her chicken soup again. If that was what it was.

"I just want to…to undo the curse. To help Dave be a man again."

"You want Batty boy be man? You crazy woman. You no see what he want?"

Lyn was thoroughly confused. The accent, the strange speech, what Mama Boo Boo was saying…

"I no fix."

"Oh."

"Papa can."

"Papa?"

"Papa. He big Papa. Papa of all. He fix Batty Boy good."

"Then he can help Dave get…erections…again?"

Mama Boo Boo shrugged. "No maybe. He fix. If he want. He big price. Lotsa money." then she turned and gazed up and down at Lyn. "Or something."

Lyn didn't catch the significance of the gaze and blurted, "How do we find this Papa person?"

"Willie take you. Willie son. He take you safe."

An hour later, a little tired, a little hungry, Dave and Lyn followed a little boy through the Jamaican jungle. They were traveling up the hills behind Kingston, had passed the rich folk area and were in the middle a steaming, seething, dripping jungle.

"You watchee snake," grinned Willie, showing his white teeth at them.

Shivering, Lyn walked under a branch which had the loops of a snake dangling from it.

They heard a leopard screaming.

Lyn gave a small cry. "I thought there were no cats in Jamaica!"

"We in jungle now. Deep jungle. Things in jungle."

The boy spoke with a mysterious attitude, and he seemed sincere.

"But you stay me. I get you Papa."

They hiked for hours, over streams, around a mountain lake where an American alligator stared at them with eyes just above the surface. And how an American alligator got up the mountain to this placid place was a mystery.

Behind the lake the trail they were following became more defined. The ground was packed by eternal footsteps, the brush was pushed back, and they had easy clearance.

They arrived at a cave and Willie stopped outside.

"Papa!" he yelled. "We come see. Papa!"

No question, Papa was in there, and they could actually feel him.

It was like knocking on a door and knowing a house was empty. No human feeling to it. Except it was the reverse. Not knocking, but the smell of a fire, the feel of human awareness leeching blearily at them.

Papa was home.

A shape in the depths. A man leaning on a stick. An old, scrawny man. Bent and shriveled. But eyes that glowed bright even from within the depths of his cave.

Nothing was said, but Willie turned. "He say okay. You go. I wait here. You go."

Apprehensively, Lyn and Dave entered the cave.

Papa was standing about fifty feet back from the mouth of the cave. When they approached him he turned and walked around a corner. They followed him and found themselves in a grotto.

It was maybe 30 feet across, and a small pond was on the right, maybe ten feet across.

Light came up from the waters, and the waters bubbled every once in a while. The light shimmied up the sides of the walls and onto the stalactites.

Around the pond was a sandy ledge, and on the far side was a pad for sleeping, a small fire, and a couple of bowls for eating, or whatever.

Papa motioned them to sit, and he sat on the other side of the fire.

It was a small fire, just twigs and a couple of branches as thick as Dave's thumb, but it gave off light and heat and never seemed to run down.

"Whachoo wan?"

He was gnarly, wrinkled, shrunken, shriveled, bald, with a large nose. His eyes were like dripping daggers, however, and there was a shrewd intelligence behind them.

"We, uh…Mama Bouchette, Boo Boo, said you could help us."

He stared, unmoving like a rock, eyes gleaming.

"We, uh, Dave, my husband, he has erectile dysfunction."

The old man frowned and tilted his head. He obviously didn't understand what erectile dysfunction was.

"He doesn't get erections any more."

Still, the old man stared, seemed to be even more puzzled.

Dave blurted. "I don't get boners." He raise a finger, then crooked it. "Limp. You understand."

The old man grinned a toothless grin and nodded.

"Why batty boy want stiff?"

That batty boy thing again. Lyn was going to have to look that up.

"He's young. We want children."

"Children with Batty?" Now the old man looked super confused.

"Look, can you help my husband or not?"

For a long second the old man said nothing, just frowned, compressed his lips, then gave the most eloquent shrug ever, a shrug that meant nothing.

"Me help." Then, handing the bowl to Dave, "Get water. No let water touch skin."

Puzzled, Dave took the bowl, took the few steps to the gleaming pond and carefully dipped the bowl into it. He returned to the old man and handed him the bowl.

There was a glass in the sand, and the old man poured the water into the glass. He was careful not to spill a drop.

He held the glass in one bony hand and told Dave, "Give me dicky dick."

Dave closed and opened his eyes, looked at Lyn, and undid his pants. He took out his dick and the old man reached for it.

Dave gave an involuntary shiver as the warm hands gripped his member.

The old man tugged, and he held the glass, and dangled Dave's dick into the glass.

The water was just the right temperature. Not cold, not hot, sort of like body temperature.

The old man lowered the glass and shook Dave's dick. There was only a little dampness on his pecker, and the old man handed Dave the glass. "You put in water. No touch water anywhere else."

Dave went to the edge of the pond. He was standing inches from the smooth surface, and he lowered the glass and poured the water back into the pond.

He started to stand up, and his feet slipped out from under him.

Retrospect he would wonder why he slipped, because at the moment it almost felt like the water was pulling him.

He fell, his feel slid into the water, then his body slid down the slope until he was totally immersed.

He came up spluttering, "Fuck!"

But he couldn't get out of the water. Every time he took a step his feet slipped and he slid back.

The old man watched with those strangely, glittering, almost all black eyes.

Lyn rushed to the edge of the pond and held out her hand.

Dave took it and she tried to pull him out. But her feet slipped and she slid down the slight slope. It felt like the water was actually pulling her.

She gave a yelp, and was totally immersed, then she was standing next to Dave, spluttering, and trying to get out of the pond.

The old man started to laugh. Not a little chuckle, or a whisper of a snicker, but a full throated roar of hysterical laughter. Gut busting, knee slapping, rolling on the floor laughter.

The more Dave and Lyn tried to get out of the pond the more he laughed.

"Please! Help us!"

Finally, the old man took off his robe, which shocked Dave and Lyn. He wasn't a man! He had a pussy! Old and gnarly and hairy and overtaken by warts.

But, pussy or not, he tossed his garment to them, and held to one end.

"Move slow, no pull."

They managed to follow his advice, and slowly they managed to extricate themselves from the pond.

They stood, dripping wet on the sand.

"Put down," the old woman motioned at her robe.

"Heysoos," and Dave shivered. He wasn't cold, but something inside him was cold. And he was hungry, and in spite of being in a pond, he was thirsty.

And now Lyn was feeling a twinge of cold deep, deep within. It was like her very ovaries were cold, and making the rest of her body cold.

The old woman stood, not touching his wet robe, and grinned.

"You no batty boy," he said to Dave. He turned to Lyn. "Now you batty boy." He started laughing again.

How Dave and Lyn made it back to the hotel they never knew.

They were shivering, miserable, and Willie had to keep pulling them along, encouraging them.

"Come…we go…go go. Hotel down there."

For hours, through the dripping jungle, past the staring wildlife, wildlife that now seemed fascinated by them, they staggered down the path.

They reached Mama Boo Boo's house and somehow, without a phone, she managed to call the taxi man.

Then, as if emerging from a terrible nightmare, awaking from a sleep filled with giant snakes and hyenas and even monster lions, they were walking through the hotel.

They looked a mess, an unhappy mess, and everybody stared at them. Then they were at their room. Falling into bed, fully clothed, not caring. Shivering. Their very spirits feeling as if they had been doused in ice water.

They slept a sleep they hadn't chosen, but which had been chosen for them.

Part Two

Dreams are fun. Flying in the sky. Seeing people we haven't seen. Fun.

Nightmares not so much fun. Can't escape the monster. somebody sawing legs off, keep sawing and sawing…

Dave had a dream mare. Not exactly a combination of the two, but close.

He was walking through a crowd with no clothes on, and his penis was six feet long. He had to carry it with both hands, and he kept falling forward, catching himself, falling forward.

People laughing. Pointing. Making rude comments. "Maybe you'll be able to make your wife happy now!" "Wait until it gets hard!"

He was laughing, but hysterically, out of control, terribly happy, even though it was a tragedy. He thought.

But what you think in dreams mirrors reality, though often in ways you don't understand.

Dave was aware that he was awake. Now how had that happened? Where was that dividing line between sleep and awake?

He was dressed, laying on the bed, and he felt funny. His clothes were all wrapped weird about him.

"Unh." He moved an arm, and it felt funny, but he couldn't understand why it felt funny.

A dull thought occurred to him: it weighs less.

He moved a leg, and his clothes, his pants, felt too big for him.

He remembered falling in the water the night before, but that wouldn't make pants stretch, would it?

And he had to pee. But…he didn't have any morning wood pain. He had a pain, a pinching within that indicated his bladder was full, but… what the fuck?

"Dave?" Lyn sounded like she had a cold. Her voice was low, and scratchy.

"Uh?"

"Something's wrong."

"Uh,,,yeah," confused, not sure what was going on.

"Dave?"

He felt her moving on the bed, and the bed jounced, more than it should have for her light body.

"AIEEE!"

She sat up.

So he sat up and looked at her.

She still had long hair, and it was tangled, but feminine. But her face was different. The angles of her cheeks, the squareness of her jaw. Her teeth looking stronger and bigger.

Then his eyes went down to her chest. Her lack of chest. She no tits!

"No!" Dave yelled and moved a hand forward to touch her, "EEIII!" he screamed. His hand was small, narrow, slender, with long fingernails. It was a woman's hand.

And, looking at his hand he saw his own chest. Now he gasped, couldn't breath for the shock. He had mountains on his chest. His pecs were now boobs, big, bulging, tipped with big, stiff nipples.

Then came a long moment where neither screamed or yelled or spoke. A moment of assessment.

Her touching his boobs, looking at her own chest, touching her chest, lifting her shorts away from her waist and looking…and pulling her shorts down…she had a big, hairy penis!

And it was rigid with morning wood!

He felt his tits, squeezed them, felt panic as the sweet electrical feeling of a stimulated sex organ lanced through his body and down to his groin.

He spun on the bed to his knees, pulled his pants down…down…and saw no dick!

Not hard, not soft, not thing! Just a smooth mons, then…a slit. A womanly slit!

Their hearts pounding, sex was forgotten in the face of this massive shift in realities.

He was a woman. He had a woman's body.

She was a man. She had a light beard, long hair a bit feminine, and… muscles.

And a cock!

And balls!

And he had a vagina.

The shock didn't lessen, but awareness slowly crept in.

Dave touched his breasts, pocked them and watched them jiggle.

She lifted her penis and held it, felt it, and it started to grow.

In spite of morning wood it had shrunk during her shock.

"I have to go to the bathroom," she spoke in a low voice, softly, amazed at the sound of herself, let alone the feel of sex organs and a male body

"I think I do, too. I feel…pressure down there."

They didn't do anything for a moment, just took their clothes off, struggling with unfamiliar fingers, him in male pants too big, her in female pants too small.

Her bra looked funny on her now, and she couldn't get her fingers back to loosen it.

"Help me," she asked.

Now it was Dave who suffered the awkwardness. His fingernails being longer he had a hard time undoing the clasps.

Finally, they were naked, and Lyn got off the bed.

She tried to slide like a girl might, being smaller and the bed being bigger, but now she was in a bigger body and she stumbled, not used to using larger limbs, more massive muscles.

Dave tried to get off the bed and almost fell, his legs were shorter and he lacked coordination. His chest was so heavy.

Then they were standing up, and they looked at each other and walked haltingly towards the bathroom.

It was a nice hotel with both a toilet and a bidet.

Lyn sat down, and Dave said, "You can stand up now."

She was trying to get her penis down past the cold lip of porcelain, and his words registered.

She stood up, off balance, and stood in front of the toilet. She held her penis and a strangled giggle came out of her masculine throat.

"How…how…"

Then the body took over and began shooting a yellow stream. It hit the wall, then the floor, got all over the toilet, then she managed to bring it under control. She listened to the water splashing and suddenly felt a strange surge of pride.

She had a dick. She had balls. And this was giving her a masculine idea of herself.

Dave sat on the bidet and waited his turn at the toilet, and suddenly the water fell out of him.

"Oh, fuck?" he whimpered. It was so different. With a cock he could push it, and aim it. Now all he could do was let it stream into the basin.

Lyn finished, waited, then, a grin, shook her cock.

"This isn't bad."

She looked at Dave, so miserable on the bidet. "You can wash yourself with that."

"How?"

She told him, reached down and helped him, and suddenly he was treated to the wonderful sensation of water spraying on his vulva. "Oh, fuck!" He looked up, amazed. "That's a sexual feeling!"

"A little practice and you'll be able to get yourself off."

He bent his head to look down, and realized how long and messy his hair was. He looked up in alarm. "I'm a mess!"

"No." Lyn understood what the change in his personality was doing to him, and she remembered how she felt as a woman. "You're just not fixed up yet. We'll fix you up."

"Fix me up…how?"

"Honey. You need to shave your whole body. You need to put on the right clothes. Most of all…you need make up."

The male in him protested. "Make up?"

"Don't be so alarmed. It's fun, and I'll help you."

"But how did this happen? How did we change like this?"

Lyn intuitively knew. "That pond last night. That glass of water was supposed to make your dick hard, but too much of it…when we fell in it changed our bodies."

"But I don't want…" he stopped. What didn't he want. There was a strong feeling of femininity in him, and it was saying something else, sighing in relief.

"I don't think I want to be a man, either, but…here we are."

"But what do we do?"

"We can go back to Mama Boo Boo. Maybe to Papa. "

"Papa was a woman!"

"And he, or she, had a healthy respect for the pond. Maybe it will change us back."

A voice in Dave whispered, *No!*

"That's a good idea," he said.

"Then let's get cleaned up. Get dressed. This body is hungry."

Dave ordered room service, two breakfasts, then headed into the shower.

Lyn showered, instructed Dave on shaving his body, then dressed quickly. She was in pants and shirt, and didn't need to bother with a bra, which was a weird relief, when the knock on the door came.

Listening to the shower, hoping Dave was doing all right, she opened the door and the big bellhop who had given her the card pushed a tray into the room.

He grinned. "Batty boy. You likee like?"

"What?" What was a batty boy?

"Big change. You have fun."

He strode out of the room, and just as he reached the door Lyn blurted, "What is a batty boy?"

He just laughed and gave a wave of his hand, then closed the door.

Dave was done shaving his body and shampooing his hair, and he came out of the bathroom rubbing his hair with a towel.

He was quite beautiful. His breasts were very large, and his nipples were stiff and excited.

He was finding the sensuality of having a woman's body.

"Sit down, honey. Let's eat."

They sat on the balcony outside and lifted the tops of the platters.

Bacon, eggs, pancakes, orange juice, a big jug of syrup.

They ate ravenously, occasionally looking up at each other.

Lyn's penis was twitching in her pants, and Dave's big breasts hung down over the glass table.

"Is it always like this?"

"What?"

"My cock! It keeps moving around, and it gets stiff, then shrinks a little, then gets stiff all over again.

Dave giggled. "You're just horny."

"I wouldn't be laughing, because there is only one cure for what I've got."

Dave's head jerked up in surprise. "What?"

"You've got a pussy. I've got a cock. Is it so hard to figure out?"

Dave was nonplussed for a moment, then he blurted, without thinking, "Not tonight…I've…I've got a headache."

Which made Lyn laugh hard. "Oh, man. Talk about the shoe being on the other foot."

Then she leaned forward a little, her strong jaw chewing on a piece of bacon. "But we both know that's a lie. At least I do, because when I said I had a headache I didn't. I just didn't want to do it with you."

"What!"

"Yep. I know you're just scared, but now I've got the big body. And I'm going to insist on making love. I want to know what it feels like to use this big, swinging dick."

Dave was stunned. It was a viewpoint of a man he had never had. She hadn't wanted to screw him, and…why? Mood? Fear? But not a headache.

"But what if I don't want to?"

They were done with breakfast now and just faced each other over the little table. Naked, hanging breasts and a cock that was pointing up through the glass at Dave.

"No. I've been a girl, and you can't pull the girl stuff on me. It's not fair."

"And it's not fair that you make me do something against my will."

"Don't worry, honey, when I'm done with you you'll feel like it."

"What do you mean?"

"I know what a girl's body likes." She grinned at him, a grin so lascivious it might have been evil, if it wasn't just lust.

"Well, I don't care. I know what I like, and I don't like the idea of having a penis in me." *Although there was something in him saying otherwise.*

"Honey, in the words of a manly man…tough."

There it was. Stalemate, with the odds in favor of the bigger, stronger body.

Then Dave said something that changed the game.

"Lyn, I'll do it on one condition."

"Oh?" She was determined that he would do it anyway, but what 'condition' did he have?

Dave stood up and Lyn's breath caught. Such a beautiful body. Even uncombed, even no make up, he was a stunner.

Dave added through the glass doors and into the apartment. He went into the bedroom, rummaged through his suitcase, the one with the male clothes, and came out with something behind his back.

He stood in front of Lyn, his hands behind making his breasts thrust forward.

Lyn had lowered her hand to her cock and was gently stroking it. It was obvious she was feeling the heat.

"I'll lay down, spread my legs, won't fight you, but you…"

"What?"

"You'll have to wear this."

Dave brought his hand out and Lyn gasped.

It was a butt plug. Small with a bulbous end, and flare on the base so it wouldn't fall into the hole.

She took it, and her hand shook a little, but whether it was fear or anticipation was up in the air.

"What is this?"

"I think you know."

"But why do you have it?"

"My big secret. I sometimes wear a butt plug."

"Up your butt."

"No place else."

Dave's female face was red, he was blushing, but he was determined to go on.

"I brought it because I wanted to confess it. No secrets between us, but now, considering the situation…you want sex, you have to do what really excited me. I know things about the male body, see, the shoe is on the other foot, and I know what's going to make you squirm and pop your cork."

She felt the little invader, studied it minutely, felt the texture and imagined it sliding into her. That bulb might be a little painful, but maybe not. there were differences between the male and female anatomy, and between a woman's hole and an asshole.

She looked up at him. "Have you ever fucked me with this in you."

"Once. It blew my mind. And I was terrified you'd find out."

"Oh, Lord," Lyn breathed. "I never suspected."

"You'll love it."

"And you'll love it when my big dick plummets into your little hole. You realize, of course, that you are officially a virgin?"

He blinked. "After fucking half my life…I'm now a virgin." The thought was weirdly intoxicating.

"Okay. How do I do this."

"Simple. Grease it up and push it in. Feel it. Enjoy it. And I want a couple of drinks. If I'm going to lose my virtue to some big, ugly stud I want to be relaxed."

"Artificially relaxed."

With that Lyn stood up. She was six inches taller than Dave, and she looked down at him, contemplating, then went into the bathroom.

Dave followed. He watched her smear the plug with lubricant. He watched as she bent over and pressed it home.

Lyn had taken dicks before, but that was in her hole, not her asshole, and this was different.

And it was the same.

A moment of light hurt as her hole stretched, then it was back together, holding the plug firmly in her.

She felt amazingly full back there, and she felt…complete. Whole. It was a good feeling, and very sensual.

She turned to Dave. "Okay, honey. Let's drink up, and I'll fix you up, and then…"

Her meaning was not lost, and Dave shivered. Even the shiver was sexual. He was a woman, what he had dreamed of and pursued all his life, and though there was a twist here, he was excited beyond belief.

In the kitchenette Lyn made the drinks. There was a recipe book on the little fridge, and she looked in it for the mixings of a Caribbean drink.

But everything needed more than she had! She needed pineapples or exotic mixers, and all she had was a fridge with Coke and Seven up, and a box with rum and tequila and bourbon and one little bottle of vodka.

"Well, this will have to hold us until we get ourselves a real mixologist." She fixed two glasses of rum and Coke and handed Dave one.

Dave looked at his small fingers holding the big glass. "You're not trying to get me drunk, are you?"

"Absolutely."

"But I'm not that kind of girl."

"You will be," she leered at him.

They sipped for a minute, then Lyn got out her make up kit.

"I'll be a little clumsy with these big hands," she noted.

Dave sat down at an inside table that resembled a vanity table, and which got plenty of light.

Lyn opened up her nail kit. "Lift your tootsies up here."

He did, and found that he had extra flexibility. That would help make up for his lack of strength.

She painted his toenails red, and he stared at the dividers as his nails dried.

Then she prepared his fingernails, glued on some fakes, and painted them red.

"This is scary," Dave said, but he was breathless. Things hidden for so long were coming to the surface.

While his nails dried Lyn began working on his face.

All the hair that was no longer on his body stood on end as he felt her use brushes, creams and other things.

She cleansed his face, primed it, and he stared at the canvas his face was becoming.

If he had had a cock it would have been straight up. Like Lyn's was.

But he didn't, so he suffered the equivalent. Heat in the groin. Heat that made his nipples tingle. He felt moisture in his groin.

"Fuck," he whispered.

"Soon, honey," Lyn whispered back.

Blush and eye shadow. Eyeliner and longer, curled lashes. Every once in awhile, while Lyn picked up a different brush, or went for a different color, he would glance at himself in the window next to the table.

There was no doubt that he was a woman, and it made his heart pound, reminding him of how his cock used to throb.

She put lipstick on him, then sat back. She smiled. A little lingerie, fix you up with all that sexy stuff, and then…"

She left it unfinished, but he finished it in his mind. *...and then she would stuff that big cock into me.* And he felt a whimper way back in his psyche.

Her bra fit him, though they did need to be just a touch bigger.

The garter went up smoothly, and the nylons unrolled onto his soft skin.

Almost done.

They had another drink, just looked at each other.

Her wanting him, her dick a monster of large proportion, She was undressed and she spread her legs and let Dave see it jutting up.

"You're very proud of that thing, aren't you."

"Weren't you of yours?"

He had to admit that.

She stood up and took a brush to his hair. She spritzed a bit of hair spray, brushed it out, gave it a soft wave that fell over his shoulders.

"Okay, honey. Are you ready to dance?"

He wasn't would never be, but…it was time.

Dave trembled as Lyn took him in her strong, muscular arms.

He felt weak, but also protected by her strength. He suddenly knew he would rely on her to protect him the rest of his life.

No more fear.

Lyn's hand came up and fondled his breasts.

Dave gasped.

Lyn bent her head and sucked on his nipples.

Dave almost cried out from the sudden pleasure emitting from his nipples, lancing through his body, making his pussy even wetter.

Lyn's hand went down to his pussy. She cupped his mons, squeezed, and Dave was light headed.

Then a finger slid inside him and he cried out.

"It's okay, honey," whispered Lyn. "I'll be gentle with you."

She picked him up, showed off her great strength, and carried him back to the bedroom.

Dave held on, could hardly breath for the fear filling him, and for the love taking over his senses.

Lyn laid him on the bed and continued kissing, fondling, touching him in all the ways that only girls know.

Dave arched his back, learned to want Lyn's fingers, then to want something more.

And, finally, finally, Lyn positioned herself between his legs, touched her huge penis to his hole, and…

Dave lay on the bed, dazed, knowing the world would never be the same again.

Next to him Lyn slept the sleep of the sexually satisfied.

Dave felt the mess leaking out of him. It was disgusting, but… enjoyable.

He had done it. He had taken it. Now he understood all those things he hadn't understood.

Sure, there were going to be times when he pretended headache, which might or might not work.

And, yes, he understood how and why a woman could be a bitch. He dreaded it, but he knew it would happen to him.

A feeling of being helpless, a second class citizen, a lack of freedom when he had to lay back and accept the hard loving of a man.

But…in the bigger scheme of things, it was all right.

In fact, it was fantastic!

"Um…are you awake?"

"Yes," Dave whispered.

"Good."

Dave turned to Lyn. "Why?" And there was a certain amount of tease in his voice.

Lyn, however, suffering a period of time to rebuild her manly juices, wasn't ready. Yet.

"I didn't tell you something earlier."

"What?" Dave reached down and touched her penis. Then he gripped it, stroked it, wished for it to be hard again.

"When the bellhop came, he said the phrase again. Batty Boy. So while you were still showering I looked it up."

"Oh?"

"I originally thought it just meant man. A bat swinging man. The bat being the penis."

"It doesn't?" He was confused. He had thought that, too.

"No. Bat is Jamaican for butt. He wasn't saying 'bat boy,' he was calling you a 'butt boy.'"

"What?" Dave sat up straight.

"That's right. A butt boy, or in the islands, a transgender. A man who wants to be a woman. To take it up the ass. Or to put it up the ass. There's a lot about this phrase that we don't understand."

Dave leaned back, lay his head on the pillow and thought about it.

"He saw me for my deeper desires. He could tell that I liked butt plugs, and that I wanted to be fucked."

"So he sent us to the witch doctor, the houngan, the one who could help you change."

"That explains so much. Things that were said, the way the old man, or woman, Papa, laughed."

"And now you are a woman. You don't get it up the butt, though we can certainly try that."

Dave turned to Lyn, his breasts heavy in his bra, feeling sexy in his lingerie, in his make up. "But for how long?"

"I think we have choice in that. We could run up to the cave, to Papa, and jump in the pool, and change back."

"But do we want to?"

"Not right now, if we're being honest. I really, really, *really* liked squirting my dick. Emptying my balls. I loved being over you, stronger than you, and yet feeling safe in you."

"And I loved it when you took me, made me feel more special than I ever had in my life."

"So, let's enjoy our vacation, even take an extra couple of weeks. Let's explore our bodies, then decide how we want to go home."

"What if I want to go home as a woman?"

"Then I'll be a lesbian for you."

They were close now, inches apart, on their sides, holding each other, and Lyn's big cock was starting to stir.

"Because it's not who's male or who is female. It's about two people loving each other, no matter what sex they are."

"Amen."

And Dave pushed Lyn back and mounted him.

END

Full Length Books from Gropper Press

Jim Camden was a manly man, until the day he crossed his wife. Now he's in for a battle of the sexes, and if he loses…he has to dress like a woman for a week. But what he doesn't know is the depths of manipulation his wife will go to. Lois Camden, you see, is a woman about to break free, and if she has to step on her husband to do it…so be it. And Jim is about to learn that a woman unleashed is a man consumed.

The Feminization Games

Feminized by a Lactating MILF!

TOTAL male to female role reversal!

Grace Mansfield

A Note from the Author!

Okay, putting together several juicy elements for this story.

Men have had a healthy interest in lactating breasts ever since, well, since they were babies!

Men have had a fascination for chastity ever since they experienced that first glorious squirt!

Men had been fascinated with women's clothes ever since they realized women didn't have dinguses.

And women…well, we've been fascinated with men ever since we realized how easy it is to control them.

Enjoy! And…

STAY HORNY!
Gracie

Part One

“Ron, What’s yours?”

“June.”

Ron smiled and tried to keep his eyes up. June was absolutely amazing. She had a slender body with a bit of booty, and a chest that entered the room before she did.

And, to top it off, she had a kind, pixie face with full lips and beautiful, blue eyes. Her hair framed her face and he felt like he was looking at the Mona Lisa.

“That’s a nice name. Can I buy you a drink?”

“Sure. As long as it’s brown liquor.”

He had to chuckle. “Right from the still.”

She laughed, and he went to the bar and bought a pair of bourbon and Cokes. He brought the drinks back, and studied her in detail. She was watching the house band and her profile was amazing. She was wearing tight jeans that showed a monkey knuckle, and a black tee with a vee neck. The vee was deep, but it didn’t need to be. Her breasts bulged and showed a deep canyon.

Ron kept his eyes up when she looked at him and accepted the drink.

“Thanks.”

“No problemo. You want to stand or sit?”

She looked askance.

“There’s a table right in the corner up there,” he pointed at the balcony. It’s hidden, behind a pillar so nobody knows it’s there.”

She looked up at a dark corner and grinned. “Are you trying to get me alone?”

“Absolutely!”

He took her hand and led her up the stairs, around the balcony, and the little table and two chairs were waiting for them.

For the next hour they sat and talked. Ignored the band, which was right below them, and became engrossed in each other.

They had a lot in common, and they were in synch conversation wise. They didn't cut each other off or talk over, it was like they were totally compatible.

And they both realized it.

They had a couple more drinks, were feeling no pain, and she blurted, "I thought you got me up here to take advantage of me!"

He didn't need a second invitation. Their chairs were already close together and he moved in, turned his chair slightly so they were facing, and he gently touched his lips to hers.

Her lips were soft and plump and he could taste her red lipstick. Her hands went down to his thighs and perched on them. She kissed him eagerly.

The music became background, and they took turns nibbling. Then she suddenly moved forward, sat on his lap and held him.

He felt those glorious, magnificent mammaries pressed against him.

He had wanted to touch them, to feel them, but he was a little afraid. She was so perfect and he didn't want to go overboard.

She whispered in his ear, "Well? Are you going to feel me up?"

Again, no second invitation, his hands rose up and gently fondled her treasures.

"Gently," she said, "I'm lactating."

He froze, and she giggled against his neck.

He kept feeling her up, his hands sliding over her breasts, feeling her erect nipples.

She waited, and he couldn't handle it. "You're…lactating? Really?"

She nodded, then she whispered. "I tell men this to see if they can handle it. I don't want to take you home and find you that you're disgusted by mother's milk.

"Oh, God," he gulped. "I'm not disgusted. It's…it's exciting."

"Then if you're a good boy maybe I'll let you have a taste."

He was totally bonered up, and she could feel it, his big penis pushing through his pants, her pants, as if trying to burst through and got into her pussy.

"What do I have to do to be considered a good boy."

"You want to be a good boy?"

"Oh, God! Yes!" He kept swallowing. His hands were so full of boob, and he was actually trembling with excitement.

"Then you just to do one thing."

"What? Anything! I'll do anything!"

She was still face into his neck and she spoke softly into his ear, "What color are my eyes?"

He knew what color they were! They were a pale blue, very magnetic, not that anybody would notice, not with her boobs being so incredible. But he had noticed.

Still he hesitated, pictured them in his mind, made sure he was right.

She continued over his hesitation. "I meet boys and they are louts. They want to fuck, they can't keep their eyes off my boobs, and they never know what color my eyes are. If you don't know, if you give the wrong answer, then I stand up and walk out and we're done. If you get the right answer then I'd like to invite you over for a nightcap, maybe talk a little. Maybe do something else."

His voice was hoarse. "Blue. Beautiful, pale blue. I checked your eyes out first because I wanted to make sure you weren't just a bimbo with boobs and no brains."

She sighed. Held him harder. "Of course if you don't want to come over for a night cap, this is a two way street, you know."

"Oh, God, are you kidding! I've never met a woman like you!"

She half stood up and reached down into his lap. She grabbed his penis through his pants and he grunted and almost squirted.

"June, you're going to make me lose control here."

She bit his ear and said, "I just want to make sure of everything. Come on, let's go have a real drink."

He followed her in his car, and she didn't try to lose him. In fact, she went slow and kept glancing back at him.

She wasn't going to lose him. Ron had had a few dog dates. And he had been a dog date for some. She definitely wasn't a dog.

She led him to a house on the edge of town, the backside opened on a hillside that sloped gently upward. She parked her Mustang and he parked his big Ford 350 and followed her into the house.

Ranch style, three bed and two bath. A big backyard, a pool and a landscaped garden, then the trek up the hill behind.

Inside it was clean and modern. The furniture was built more for comfort, and less for looks.

"Have a seat and I'll make you something you;'ll never forget," she winked at him.

He plopped onto the couch and admired the pool through the big sliding doors. He heard her clinking glasses in the kitchen, then she came out with two big, drinking glasses. This girl meant business.

"What's this?" asked Ron, holding the pinkish colored liquid.

"Try it, then ask."

He sipped, blinked, and took a gulp. "Wow!"

"Brown Derby, with good bourbon. It's got honey syrup and grapefruit juice."

He gulped again, and she sat down in a chair opposite him and kicked off her heels.

They sipped, and it was a purely enjoyable moment. Just enough liquor to get high, not so much they were stupid. And their chemistry was really working.

In the bar it had worked, but sometimes, take the people out of the bar, and chemistry changes. Theirs didn't. They talked, traded quips, and everything they said just seemed to fit together.

Halfway through the drink she lifted her feet to his lap. She was wearing short stockings under the jeans, and he felt the silky smooth material. Very sexy.

"Rub my feet and I'll let you drink from my tits."

She was still testing him, it was in her eyes, make sure he's worthy of real milk.

He sipped, put his glass down and set to rubbing. He took his time, working his fingers into the crevices and moving his thumbs over the pads.

She sighed, sipped, and sat back.

"This makes my pussy wet," she whispered.

He said nothing, just smiled.

"I'm not going to fuck you tonight. It's a first date, you know. I just want to get to know you. We get along, but I want to know more about you until I let that big honker into my pussy. I will play with you, however. I want to know about you, and nothing tells a girl more about a man than a cock."

"As long as you don't get mad if I have an accident."

"Accidents are good." She leaned forward and pulled her tee shirt off.

They were even bigger without the tee. The bra was a nursing bra and had thick pads to absorb her milk.

Her nipples were so big they could be seen through the pads.

"Now he couldn't talk. He was mesmerized. He worked his fingers along her soles and stared at her breasts.

"You've really got it bad," she grinned.

"I know. I'm sorry."

"Don't be. If you're smart enough to observe the world, meaning the color of my eyes, then I don't mind if you're a kinky, little bitch."

Her words were stated in a significant manner, and he looked up at her, but she was just smiling.

For long minutes he rubbed, stared, gulped, and his penis felt totally trapped inside his pants.

They finished their drinks, and now they were loopy. She stood up and took off her bra. Her large milk sacks hung down, her nipples were engorged, ready to squirt.

"Take your pants off," she requested, eyeing him like he was a steak and she was a wolf.

He stripped his pants off, hardly aware of what he was doing, staring at her charms, and his penis sprang out.

She walked around to the back of the couch. "Scoot down just a little."

He slumped on the couch.

She leaned over the back and dangled her breasts over his face. She lowered herself slightly, and the nipples were right in front of his eyes.

"Well?"

He moved slowly, opened his mouth and placed it over her nipples. He sucked, and the sweet, warm taste of fresh milk entered his mouth.

A lot of milk.

She rested on the back of the couch while he fed, and explained about lactation.

"My ex wanted me to lactate. He was a freak. He gave me pills that would cause the milk to flow, and I liked it. I have to be milked several times a day, and I love it. I love the feeling of a hot mouth sucking on me. It's probably like the feeling you get when somebody sucks on your hot pecker."

She gripped his dong and started jacking him.

"My breasts grew bigger, and I need somebody to help milk them. Most men are in it for a kick, but they chicken out after a while, especially at the thought of a long term relationship. Mind you, I don't want to get married, but I need a man to help me, to suckle me, to make me feel good. There might be an occasional booty call in it for you, but, maybe not. I'm not a big sex freak, but getting my tits sucked is sex enough. It's like I get brought to a peak and left there, and who wants to give that up? So I want you to suckle, often, and in return I'll play with you. I'll bring you close. Sex? I don't know. I don't mind the mess of milk all over the place, but I hate it when I have this thick good inside me, dripping out all over the place. Are you enjoying yourself?"

Ron was going back and forth between her breasts, one, then the other. Equal time.

She leaned further forward and he had to adjust his position to keep sucking, but she placed her mouth on his dong.

His cock jerked in her mouth, and she squeezed the base with her hands. "Don't squirt, honey. Enjoy the frustration. Get horny for me. Get so horny you fall in love and…stay in love.

His heart was pounding, he was shivering, he wanted to squirt in the worst possible way, but she meant business. She wasn't going to let him.

They lay like that, twined like that, her over him in a 69 that only went from breast to cock, and he felt like he was riding an explosion, without the explosion.

An hour later she sighed and let him go. He had come close several times, but she had kept him under control. She was good, and she sensed when he was going to lose it, and stopped him.

"Oh, God," he whimpered. His penis was an angry, red rod, throbbing and dripping pre-cum.

"Thanks, honey," she said, walking back around the couch. "I'm empty now. "If you want to spend the night I've got a guest room. I'll need you to milk me for breakfast, whether you stay or go. Okay?"

That was a moment in which he noted a certain nervousness in her manner. He didn't understand that he had pleased her, more than any other man, and she didn't want him to go.

"I'll spend the night," he said. "I don't want to drive with alcohol in my system."

She showed him to the guest room, gave him a new toothbrush. There was a bathroom across the hall, and he should take a bath, or just jump in the pool if he wanted. And she didn't care if he walked around naked.

He opted for the pool.

She went to bed and he went out and slid into the pool. The water was perfect, the night was warm, and he watched while her bedroom light went out.

His cock felt incredible in the warm water. He sliced through the water and loved the feeling of his cock acting like a keel. He imagined himself a porpoise, sliding through the water after a boat. The boat was named June.

He stepped out of the pool and stood in the night air, dripping dry, his lust projected mightily. He wondered how he was going to sleep after this?

Where had this woman been all his life?

He had had girlfriends, but the relationships had never lasted. Usually he was just too kinky. Most women didn't like kink.

June seemed to like it. but…he would see.

"Morning, boner butt!" She showed her teeth in a big smile as she gripped his blankets and pulled them off. She was wearing nothing, but her breasts were big and full. Drops of milk formed at the tips and dripped.

He didn't try to hide his excitement. But he did have to pee.

He rolled off the ned, stood up, and she grabbed him and kissed him. A horny, hungry kiss that sucked at his soul.

She gripped him. "I need you to milk me."

His voice was a little strangled. "I need to pee first."

"Okay," she pulled him across the hall and into the bathroom. She held him and aimed him, and he let go with a sigh of relief.

Halfway through the sound of his pee tinkling in the bowl, still holding on to him, she began kissing him.

It was awkward, and exotic, and erotic. He almost lost his balance, but he managed to finish his work. She held his cheek with one hand, studied him. "Is everything okay?"

"Well, I am a little thirsty."

A look of happy glee crossed her face.

She pulled him into the kitchen and handed him a milking bottle. "You can do both my tits at the same time."

It was perfect, sitting at the table and sucking with his mouth and working the trigger of the bottle.

She breathed deeply and leaned against him.

It took fifteen minutes, fifteen minutes of bliss, for him to empty her.

"Oh, thank you. It can get a little painful if they get too full, and I certainly don't want to go dry."

She began making breakfast then.

Bacon and waffles and a glass of Coke. The Coke was good for hangovers, but neither of them really felt unduly hung over.

"So how are you doing?" she asked as they munched.

"I'm in heaven," he answered happily.

That was the right response. She was feeling a little nervous. Most men had bugged out by this time, and she didn't want him to leave.

"Are you going to get tired of milking me?"

"Are you kidding?"

She relaxed even more.

"What do you want to do today? It's a weekend. Want to go

somewhere?"

"How about a museum?"

"Perfect! But, uh…can I ask…how long between milkings?"

"Technically, three hours, but I've found that four is best for me. Four and my breasts start to ache a little, and that's when it feels best to get milked."

"If we make a day of it we'll have to find a place for me to suckle."

"I've got a van. It was my husband's. It's a work van with no windows. I've fixed it up for traveling, and…would you mind driving a van?"

"A van is fine. Where is it?"

"In the garage. Let's get dressed and I'll show you."

He had his clothes from the night previous, and he needed a change. He didn't like the smoke smell from the bar. So he put his clothes on and decided they would have to stop by his place for a quick change.

When she came down the hallway she took his breath away.

She was wearing short shorts that definitely showed her pussy. She was wearing a tight top that didn't show cleavage, but did hug her breasts so tight you could see every inch of her shape.

"I've got a thinner bra on. We'll have to watch out that I don't leak."

"I can watch your tits," he offered with a smile.

She loved his flirt and gripped his groin and kissed him. Then she backed off and wiped her lipstick off his mouth.

The van was an older Chevy, but it was in fine condition. The paint job was shabby, but when Ron turned the key the smooth purr made him smile.

The back had a cooler, a pail with a toilet seat on top of it, and two thick plywood sheets folded down from each side to make a big double bed.

"Wow! This is nice."

"Let's stop for some ice and Cokes and things, we can go to the beach after the museum."

"Sounds good. I have to stop at my place first, change of clothes, pick up a swim suit."

"I've got all that stuff here. My ex is about your size. Come on."

Ron followed her to the master bedroom. It was big, and it had two walk in closets. One on one side of the room, and one on the other. She took him into her ex-husband's and rummaged through the clothes.

The first thing Ron noticed was that her ex had a lot of pink clothes, and some of them were…weird.

Her ex had pink shoes with two inch heels. He had regular slacks, and a couple of pair of pink slacks. He had regular shirts, but he also had shirts with puffy sleeves, sequins, and…a couple that were pink.

But that wasn't the worst of it.

"You know, if you're going to wear his clothes you might as well try on some of his underwear."

"Uh, I don't—"

"You'll like this." She held up a pair of underwear that was just strips of cloth and an elastic cock ring.

"What?"

"Come on, try it. Billie used to love this."

He had misgivings, and was actually blushing, but he lifted first one leg, then the other, and she pulled the underwear up his legs.

She put the C-ring around his cock and snapped it shut. It was like a little hand holding him, and it felt really good.

"I'm going to have a boner all day."

"Good. I'll be dripping all day." She handed him a pink jumpsuit with shorts.

"I can't wear that!"

"Of course you can."

"It's pink!"

"Pink is the new black."

"How will I pee?"

"Plan ahead. Or just pull up a leg and aim carefully."

"But…but…"

But she bullied him into it.

It buttoned up the back, of all places, so he couldn't do the zipper. She did the zipper, turned him around and made him look in a mirror.

“Isn’t that gorgeous?”

“Well, uh…don’t I look a little feminine?”

The jumpsuit was loose on him, and it could have passed for male, but… it was pink. Not a manly color.”

“Nope,” she lied. “You looked beautiful. The way a man should look. “Now if you were wearing high heels, showing off that beautiful ass of yours, but…” she shrugged.

He stared at her with wide eyes. High heels?

But she just grinned like it was all a joke. “Tell you what. He had a light coat and you can wear that.”

She took out a thin jacket. It reached to down to his thighs, leaving only a strip of pink showing underneath.

He stared at himself in the mirror. Yeah, that would work, but…

“That’s good. Let me grab a swim suit, I’ve already got one for you, and we’ll head on out.”

Five minutes later Ron was steering the van down the street. He felt very self conscious with his pink shorts showing, but he cold handle it. Heck, he’d have to handle it.

The weird thing was that his cock was on display. It was hard, and it showed prominently through the thin, pink material.

Still…

They parked at the museum parking lot and entered. There were lots of people there, and June hugged his arm, pressed her big tits against his arm, and they meandered through the crowd.

And he realized that nobody was staring at him, pointing at him, or laughing at him.

“They’re all jealous,” June pointed out when he observed this. “They wish they could wear beautiful clothes and make them work.”

The museum was a gas, but it wasn’t a big museum, and they were out by eleven. Two hours. June’s boobs weren’t full yet.

They drove through town and headed for the beach. It was a beautiful day, perfect for some waves, and they found a secluded spot up the coast.

Only a couple of cars were parked alongside the road.

"Should I do a little feeding before we go? Give us longer out on the sand?"

June was happy with that and they adjourned to the back area. It was dark back there, and he could barely see her. She laid with her upper body against the side of the van, and he laid next to her, in her arms, suckling on her breasts.

God, he loved it. He loved the big, soft feel of her boobs. He loved the stiff, hot feel of her nipples in his mouth. It made his penis so totally erect; he couldn't even remember feeling this hard ever.

For fifteen minutes he traded back and forth, then she indicated that she was good to go.

"Okay, you have my suit?"

"Sure, slip out of the jumpsuit."

He did, and she pulled a pair of swim trunks up his legs. He was still wearing the C-ring because she wanted him to wear it.

He wasn't about to argue. Feeling so horny, having a beautiful woman play with him, he was glad to wear the C-ring.

"Better wear your jacket. It's windy out there."

While she slipped into a bikini he pulled on the jacket, then they pushed the door back, he picked up the cooler and she the umbrella, and they set off.

It was just a short walk over some tall dunes, and they were there. It was warm, a perfect day, and Ron wondered, "Wonder why there aren't more people here?"

"Not their kind of beach," murmured June, which was a weird thing to say.

Down the beach were a couple of couple playing volleyball. In the other direction were several people laying on big beach towels. but they had their little spot pretty much to themselves.

Ron screwed the umbrella into the sand and June laid out two towels. Then Ron panicked. He took off his thin jacket and saw what he was wearing.

A pink Speedo. Stretchy. And his cock, enhanced by the C-ring stood out for all to see.

"Oh, my God!"

"Sit down," murmured June, a slight smile on her face.

"This is too much! This is too pink!"

"It's perfect. Now sit down."

She actually reached up and grabbed his penis, sticking right through the material of the speedo, and made him sit.

Then she kissed him.

He was caught between lust and panic. He looked like…like a fag or something! But her lips were so delicious, and her hand was rubbing his boner, up and down, turning him on even more.

"There's nobody here," she whispered.

"But what if somebody comes?"

"Then they'll see a man in a pink suit who's very excited."

"But what if…"

She just kept kissing him, playing with him, keeping him down so he couldn't jump up and run away.

It took a while, but he finally relaxed. A little.

They lay on the blankets, and she opened the cooler. "I made some special Coke," she said.

She unscrewed a plastic bottle and handed it to him.

He sipped, and harsh liquor poured down his throat.

"Oh, fuck!" And, in spite of his apparel, he grinned. "Bourbon! My favorite fruit!"

"And you can drink it all. I'm the designated driver tonight."

"Really?"

"Absolutely."

So Ron sat in his pink swim suit and sipped bourbon and the sun passed slowly overhead.

A plastic bottle later he was brave enough to risk the waves, and anybody seeing his pink suit.

They walked down to the waves, frolicked for a while, then Ron saw some people coming over the big dunes.

"Uh oh," he whispered.

"He's got no suit on," she observed of one of the two men coming over the dune.

"What? Wait! He's naked!"

"Of course he is."

Ron stared at June.

"That's the kind of beach it is."

It hit him then, her earlier remark about 'not their kind of beach,' it wasn't a family beach. It was for nudists, and, apparently, watching the two men come down the face of the dunes, good for gays and…and whoever else wished to use it.

It dawned on him. Nobody would care about his pink suit. He wouldn't stand out; he would blend in.

In fact, they would assume he was, not gay, but…maybe gay. Maybe some other kink.

Something inside him loosened up.

Suddenly he didn't care what people thought of him. He was okay. It was okay.

They walked back up the sand to their umbrella and sat down on the towels. Ron sipped some more bourbon, and, for a change, he was sort of at peace with the world.

"You doing okay?"

"Yep," he blurted, then found himself grinning.

"So let's talk."

He turned to her. She was never more gorgeous, her breasts bulging out of her bikini, her blue eyes staring at him, her hand on his cross legged thigh.

His cock stuck out rudely, pushing the pink, and it was okay. Hell, everything was okay.

"What do you want to talk about?"

"I want to talk about you and me."

Not even that statement unnerved him. He was so comfortable with her.

"What about you and me?"

"Ron?" Her hand slid up his thigh and brushed against the side of his cock.

"Yes?"

"I want to do things with you."

"Well, sure." He leered. "I want to do things with you."

"Do you know why my husband left me?"

"He was stupid?"

She chuckled. "Maybe. Probably." Then she grew serious. "He left because I wanted to do things with him, and he just couldn't handle it."

"What kind of things?" his brow furrowed.

"Things like having him wear kinky underwear. Making him milk me all the time."

"What a dope. How could he pass up on that?"

She smiled and continued, "I wanted him to wear a chastity device, I wanted him to not even have a chance to lust after somebody else. I wanted to control him totally."

Now Ron was silent.

"I wanted him to wear what I told him to. It made him horny, super horny, but he couldn't handle it. I wanted all sorts of things, but you know how you felt when you discovered you were going to wear pink?"

He nodded.

"He felt like that all the time, but he could never get over it. He couldn't bring himself to live life the way I wanted him to. But I think you can."

"I can?"

"I got you into pink on your first day. Look at you. A pink suit with a C-ring showing your cock off for the world to see. You can do it. And I want you to do it."

Ron suddenly understood everything. How she had manipulated him in the closet into pink. What she had said to get him to wear, and be comfortable in pink. The C-ring. The beach.

Just as she had tested him at the bar, asking him what color her eyes were, she was still testing him.

Could he do it?

And it was obvious what the rewards were if he could. He would get to relieve her breasts of milk. She would play with him. but…he wouldn't get to cum.

"But I want to have sex!"

"I know you do. But you're going to find it's more fun to want than to get."

He stared at her, his heart pounding, thoroughly excited by what she was saying.

"But—"

She shushed his lips with a finger. "Listen, honey. You've already decided. I could tell what kind of a man you were from the first time you stared at my boobs. So let me tell you what we're going to do."

He waited.

"First, I'm going to stroke your cock to a cum. I'm going to squeeze your balls and stroke your shaft. I'm going to play with your glans until you squirt. Then I'm going to put a chastity tube on you."

He gulped.

"Then I'm going to put a butt plug in you. A plug with a ring on it. I've got a leash, and I'm going to attach that leash to your butt plug, and I'm going to take you off this beach the way you want to go. You're going to be mine, honey. I'm going to own you. You're going to come home with me and I'm going to tease you and deny you and tantalize you and…and you'll even be able to sleep with me. We'll have a pure love because you'll always be excited for me, and never get to lose that excitement. It'll be the purest kind of love, and I know you: it's the kind of love you want."

Ron sat there, her hand now on his penis. She was going to make him squirt, then never let him squirt. It was a frightening idea…that he loved.

"Okay, honey, before I do this I need you to do one thing."

"What?" his voice croaked.

"Nod your head. Say yes. You do that and the paradise begins. Nod."

It only took a brief second. A moment while things darted through his mind, then settled down.

He gave a nod.

Part Two

She didn't let him cum right away. She knew her business, she knew how to make a man go crazy with desire.

She scooted over to him and pulled his pink suit down and exposed him. There were more people on the beach then, but nobody seemed to care. They would glance, grin, and go on about their own business.

She used her fingernails on his shaft and squeezed his balls. She ran her palm around his head and even leaned down to take his head briefly in her mouth.

Ron was in the heaven of sex, but the hell of being kept on edge. He kept lurching his hips, but she would smile and slow down and keep him getting closer and closer.

His mind was becoming frayed and he began to blubber and beg.

She smiled and kept edging him. "Enjoy it, honey. It's just a taste of what's coming your way."

A couple came over to watch. The man was in good shape, but his face was a little long. He had slabs for cheeks and his teeth were long. The woman was a knock out. Long hair and perky breasts.

"Wow, how long are you going to keep him there?"

"Until he breaks," June snickered.

Ron's face turned crimson with mortification, but June didn't stop, and he was caught, no way he was going to stop this action.

"Are you lactating?" asked the woman.

"I am. Would you like to suck?"

She shook her head, but the man cleared his throat.

"Would you like to suck my tits?"

The man looked at his girlfriend nervously.

"I should be upset, but…it's sort of kinky. Go ahead.

They assumed a strange posture. June playing with Rod while leaning back, the newcomer kneeling next to her and sucking the milk out of her tits.

"Equal time, honey," cautioned June. "Do both breasts."

Rod was squirming, wanting to cum, and yet feeling jealousy.

"Would you like to suck his cock head? She asked the woman.

"I don't know. Do you think I should, honey?"

"The man, his mouth full of June's big mammaries, nodded and made a grunting sound that was in the affirmative.

She got down and gave his head a gobble, and people from around the beach were starting to really notice. A couple of couples came to watch, and the sight of four people playing with each other had the men with their hands in their pants and stroking.

But while this was happening June kept her mind on what she was about. She kept stroking and choking, slapping and tapping, and Ron knew the end was coming.

When it did come it was odd. He didn't cum with a huge bang that ended his world, he just overflowed. There was an orgasm in there somewhere, but…it wasn't strong. That can happen when a guy is stimulated too long.

He lay there, gasping, his semen all over her hand.

"Okay, kids," murmured June happily. "He came, so the show's over."

Nobody was unhappy, even though they wanted more, and they all backed off, and the crowd began to disperse.

"Wow. That was cool," said the woman who had sucked on Rod's weenie. "You want me to do that to you, hon?"

Her boyfriend was grinning. "I don't know. Maybe."

They walked away discussing it.

Her and Rod now alone, June took a chastity tube out of her purse and fit it to him. She pushed and pulled his now slack balls and cock through the ring, then slipped a small tube over his glans and down his shaft.

He was so limp it was actually a little difficult. His was a worm that was just a blob.

Click. She locked it.

His cock didn't react, it was so emptied.

He was laying on his back and she pushed him, made him roll over. "Scootch up."

Groaning, just wanting to go to sleep, Ron managed to bring his knees up. His butt now in the air, she produced a plug. It was silver colored and had a pink diamond in the base.

"Just relax honey. If you tighten up it could hurt."

She put the plug to his anus, wiggled it slightly, then just popped it in. Quick.

He grunted and flattened out on the blanket, and realized he was full.

"Feels good, eh?"

He nodded, tried to figure why it felt so good.

Here's the odd thing: he was empty, but there was a horniness still in him. He had been drained, but he had been brought so high that he still had a residual desire in him. All his senses were on high and the thing in his butt…he couldn't figure it out.

There was a part of him that wanted to say 'no.'

But she had horned him up so well that the bigger part wanted more.

She slapped his ass. "Go rinse off in the waves."

"I want to sleep,"

She pressed on the pink diamond and wiggled the plug.

"Oh, fuck," he whined.

Then she tapped on the diamond with a knuckle. Hard.

"Oh, shit!" It was like an earthquake inside his sexual apparatus. Horny or not, that could not be ignored!

He got up and stood on unsteady legs. His breathing was ragged, and June laughed. "Go, sweetheart. Rinse all that cum off." As she spoke she licked her fingers, and he realized something: she had used his own cum to lubricate the butt plug.

That made his penis wiggle inside the tube.

He staggered off down the sand.

People saw him coming. They laughed and pointed at the chastity tube. These were the same people who had watched, or even partaken, of the orgy just minutes ago.

Half embarrassed, half not caring, and half horny, Ron plodded past them.

When he was past he heard the snickers and giggles as they saw his butt plug.

He stepped into the ocean and sighed. The water was refreshing, a bit cold, but exactly what he needed to wake him up after his cum induced lethargy.

He lay on his back for a long minute and just sighed.

The way his cum had just dribbled. It had not exploded like he wanted, it had just poured out of him, and then, nothing but an almost relief, his desire still pushing at him.

How weird.

He stood up and walked out of the water.

Now fully aware, still horny but no longer in a sexual haze, he walked up the beach.

People chuckling, and now he was embarrassed. Now he started to care.

He reached the blanket and June told him to sit.

He sat, and felt the thrill of having the ground push his plug deeper.

She handed him a drink. "Suck it up, honey," she laughed. "Get used to it. This is your life from now on."

He glugged the drink, and she was okay with that.

"It's a celebration," she kissed him. "We're celebrating your belling."

"What do you mean?"

"Have you ever heard the story of the cat and the mice?"

"Where the mice sneak up on the cat and put a bell on his collar so they'll always know when he's coming?"

"That's the one."

She had one more thing in the cooler, and she brought out a bell. It wasn't one of these little rattle balls, it was an actual bell, and when she swung it back and forth it made a clear, ringing sound.

She reached forward and lifted his chastity tube. At the tip of the tube, just over the pee hole, was a small ring. She hooked the bell to that and sat back with a smile.

"What's this?" He knew, but he couldn't understand. His mind was truly being blown.

"I've just belled you."

He stared at the bell on the end of his chastity tube, and he realized something. "This thing, this chastity thing…it's metal."

"Absolutely. And the lock is a real lock. No getting out of it. And there are little points of intrigue on the inside. You won't be able to back your cock out, jack it, then put it back in."

As she spoke his body started to react. He felt his penis stirring, and he realized: *he was actually getting turned on by this! He had just cum, but…he was. trying to get hard!*

June chuckled and made him another drink. She handed it to him. "It's going to be a wild and crazy week until you get used to it. You might even end up begging me to take it off, but…nope. So you get to drink all you want for this week, then we'll put you on a diet, and you'll have to ask me for any alcoholic relief.

He could feel the shock in his mind. He could feel his overwhelming amazement. He was locked! He was fucked, if you considered the invader in his butt, and…she held the key!

"What about…what about…"

"What about what?"

"The butt plug?"

"Isn't that fun? Doesn't it feel good?"

"Uh…"

"I'll take that out every once in a while, but right now you're in training."

"In training for what?"

"Well, honey, I should probably tell you something."

"What?" he felt like the world was spinning around him, and it wasn't just the alcohol.

"Come to my nipples while we talked. They didn't empty me, and I feel pretty full.

He laid against her, suckled on her, and now was oblivious to the stares

—stares which he now knew were jealousy—from people on the beach directed to them.

She held his head and sighed as he fed, then, "You know how I told you I don't really like to have sex? I don't really enjoy the feeling of a penis in me?"

"You didn't really tell me…" He looked up from her dripping nipples.

"But I told you a little, and the hint was all there."

"Uh…yeah."

"Well, it's true. I don't enjoy the feeling of being screwed. I don't like a man hovering over me, ruling me, controlling me, whatever you want to call it. Some women love it, live for it, but to me it's demeaning. It takes away my worth, my power. I become a victim to a man."

"But—"

She put a finger to his lips and shushed him. "Suck, honey. That's what you're here for. And listen."

He bent back to the task of emptying her, and finally began to realize how truly large her boobs were.

"What I do enjoy is wearing the dick."

"You…like…"

She pushed his head back to her nipple.

"Yes. There is absolutely nothing like wearing a strap on and being the one in charge. I love the look in the man's eyes when I take him. I love how he stares at me afterwards, like he's my property. Like I own him."

"But I don't think I want somebody doing that to me!"

Again, she just guided his head down to her erect nipples.

"I know. All men are the same. They say they don't want it. But they have a hidden desire. Deep inside they want to know what it's all about. Inside all that manly swaggering every man lives to be penetrated, to be owned. It reassures them, lets them know their place in the universe."

"But…I don't…"

"Now drink up, honey. I'm in charge, and there's a lot more we have to do. Drink up, and I'll put some bourbon in another bottle of Coke for you. We've got to head for home."

He looked up, and she let him. Her tits were feeling empty now, and she handed him a bottle of Coke.

He took the bottle and sipped. It tasted strange after milk, but he washed the warm taste of milk away with cold Coke that had an extra kick.

There was a fear in him. Almost a terror, or was that pounding in his chest his heart crying out its love?

She drove back to her home. She would almost always drive from this point on. He sat in the passenger seat and felt his butt plug absorb the bumps in the road, transmit those bumps into little thrills in his anus and his sex.

And he wanted to suck on her tits again.

He knew he was hooked. He knew he couldn't fight back. And, there was a part of him that wanted to protest, to undo this play. It was a small part, though.

Now his cock was in full protest. It had only been an hour or so since he came, but it was pushing against the insides of the cage, trying to unfurl, feeling the frustration of being stopped.

"How are you doing?" she asked just before they arrived at her house.

"I'm..okay."

"Good. And don't worry, honey. You'll go through some doubts, maybe even a little anger, but then it'll all settle down. You've come to love what I'm doing to you. You'll find it the most exciting thing in the world."

"Oh." He stared at her house as they came up the driveway.

It was so white bread, and she was anything but.

As she had promised, she had hooked a leash to his butt plug, a little ring just below the diamond, and she had led him off the beach.

Now she stopped in the drive and said, "Stay here."

Curious, he stayed in his seat while she got out and walked around to his side. He watched her breasts jiggle and wanted to go to them.

She opened the door and held the leash in her hands. "Give me your ass."

He gulped, but did so. Part of him wanted to jump out and run off screaming. But he had agreed, and there was an excitement that seemed to be taking over his common sense. He knelt on the passenger seat and pointed his white cheeks at her, and she hooked the leash to his butt plug.

"You know," she said as she stepped back and let him out. "I used to use a leash on the cock. But I love that bell so much, and I do seem to have more control when I leash to the plug."

It dinged when he climbed out of the van. His face bright red he listened to the dinging as she led him to the walkway.

"After all, I tug on the package and the worst that could happen is you would lose your manhood. I tug on your butt plug and it feels like your whole insides could fall out.

She gave him a tug, and he had to agree. He yipped and she laughed.

There were tall bushes on the sides of the walkway so he couldn't be seen below the waist, but still…he was out in the open, people could see him, like they had on the beach.

But the beach was private, this was not so private.

And to make matters worse the bell dinged with every step he took.

Ding…ding…ding…

He stopped walking.

"Come on, honey."

"Can't we take this bell off?"

"Nope." She slapped his ass and made him jump. Not from the shock of the slap, which was considerable, but from the way it made him feel the plug inside him.

Every step he dinged, and every step he could feel the plug rubbing on his prostate. The perfect marriage of heaven and hell.

He opened the door and started to head for the kitchen, but reached the end of his leash.

"Unh!" he groaned. He could probably just run and it would pop out, but it would hurt first, then she would just put it back in.

Realizing that, that was the moment he started to wonder at himself. Why was he doing this?

At first he had been doing everything because of the heat in his loins, the tremendous desire he had for this most perfect of women. But now, having cum, he had a moment of doubt.

June must have seen it on his face, because she pulled him to her. She kissed him, she held his cage with one hand and pulled up on his leash very gently with her other hand. She had him massage her breasts with his hands.

"Honey, it's okay. Just go with it. I guarantee, it'll only take a couple of hours for your juices to build back up, and then it'll be fine. You won't want anything but this."

She led him into the kitchen and made him a drink.

An hour later he sat on the lounge chair next to her pool and sipped. For an hour she had kissed him, played with him, and had him suckle her. He was a little loopy, a little desperate, a little irritated, and he felt the wonderful feeling of being filled back there.

He reached down and lifted his cage, made the bell ding.

He had been belled. And chastised and plugged. He hated it and he loved it. "Wait," she had said. "Wait and it'll be all right."

He felt like chalk was screeching on the blackboard of his mind. But the screech was sexual in nature and…he loved it.

"Rod? Honey? Could you come to the bedroom?"

He stood up, making his bell ding and his cock struggled. He walked across the patio. Ding! Ding! Ding! Each step accompanied by a sexual urge in his backside.

He walked into the house and down the hallway. Ding! Ding! Ding! His cock giving a lurch with each step. His balls felt like they were full again.

He was feeling his sexual urge rise. She had been right. It had only been a couple of hours, and he was feeling it.

"Yes?" He stepped into the bedroom.

"Take off your swim suit and use this." She handed him a bottle of Nair.

Rod didn't have much hair, and he didn't like a lot of hair. Except on his head, of course.

He stepped into the shower and slathered the goo on his body. He stood, waiting, and June waited outside the shower. No talking, just waiting, just absorbing the new sensations of a new reality.

Then his skin started to heat up. It felt like a prickling sort of sunburn, and he turned on the shower. Cold at first, it countered the heat, then the warm water started and he was fine.

Watching his hair drizzle off his body and circle the drain.

And his skin felt different now. It felt…electric. Like the hair had been a shield, and now the shield was gone and he could feel the real reality.

He stepped out and she toweled him off. "Oh, this is gorgeous. She shook his tube and the bell dinged and she giggled. "I love this."

She held his package and pulled him into the bedroom. She had his clothes on the bed.

"Can't I go back to my apartment and pick up some clothes?"

"Negative, honey butt." She helped him into culottes, then a sheer blouse. Both were pink, and he shivered as he looked at himself in the mirror.

"Come with me." She led him out to the dining room and had him sit at the big table.

"Sit back and put your feet up here."

He slouched and raised his feet, and she carefully trimmed his nails. Then she began painting them.

His cock was really struggling now. The further away from his cum the more his cock struggled, and it felt good, and…it felt…terrible. Terribly bad in a good way.

He groaned and she glanced up at him and smiled.

She painted his nails a bright red, put lacquer on them to harden them and give them a glossy look.

"Fuck," he whispered to no one.

"Now the hands."

"Really?"

She leaned forward and held his package. "Do you feel that?"

He stared at her.

"That's your Mexican jumping bean. That's your heart pounding. That's your love for me and all that I'm doing."

She said nothing more, just pulled his hand out on the table, spread his fingers, and began prepping them.

His mind was spinning, and his heart was throbbing. He was dazed and confused as he watched her put fakes on his fingers and paint them to match his toes.

She hummed to herself, focused on the task, then whispered, "We're going to have so much fun. You're going to take hormones, and if your breasts don't come in big enough I'll give you some implants. You'll learn how to apply your own make up, and we'll go everywhere and do everything. Sometimes they'll think we're lesbian lovers, and always you will be feeling this wonderful, sexual desperation. You'll want to cum worse than you ever have in your life, but every moment you want to cum is a moment deeper in love with me."

He held up his hands and stared at them. She had given him long fingernails, and he would have to learn how to do things with his hands all over again.

The thought percolated into his skull: she was going to feminize him. Terrifying. Why wasn't he running?

He looked up, and she had the lipstick ready.

"But—"

She pinched his cheeks with one hand and rolled on lipstick with the other.

"There's a heavy plumping agent in this lipstick. Your lips will burn for a while, then they'll be big and fat and oh, so kissable.

She told him to sit and wait, and she left the room.

He looked at himself in the reflection on the big picture window. He didn't recognize himself.

She returned, and she was wearing high heels. They were almost the same height, but the heels made her taller than him. She handed him a pair of black Mary Janes.

"You'll wear these."

He put them on and stood up, his cock giving a ding!

She was taller than him.

She moved against him, pressed her body against him.

Now he gave a light sob. He didn't understand. He had been drinking all day, feeding from her breasts so much he wouldn't need dinner.

She held him, let him cry, and just soothed him. Patted his back, and finally lifted his leash and jiggled his plug.

Then she brushed his hair with her fingers, brushed it out and even gave it a feminine twist.

He groaned. It felt so good. It felt like a big load was being shaken in his balls.

“Okay, honey. You’re warmed up enough. Shall we seal the deal?”

He knew what she wanted, the same way any woman knows what a man wants.

She led him down the hallway. Ding! Ding! Ding!

She pushed him over the side of her bed and pulled his culottes down.

He was exposed, and he knew…he knew…

She removed the butt plug, and he suddenly felt empty. He had only had it in for a couple of hours, but he missed it.

“Don’t worry, honey. We’ll put it back in, right after I’ve deposited my load in you.”

He lay on the bed, his feet on the floor, his chest pressed down, his butt open and his chastity dangling.

She went to a dresser drawer and took out a strap on. Smiling at him, she fastened the harness, then screwed a big dildo onto the front plate.

He lay there, his breathing accelerating. Was he really okay with this? was he really going to let her do this?

She moved behind him and nudged up against him, and he had his answer. A sudden pain, then he groaned and arched his back, trying to get his ass away from her.

A minute later he was pushing back.

Epilogue

June slept, her snores soft and more like sighs. She was content.

Rod lay next to her in his mess. June had squeezed the balls of her strap on at the end, and he had been filled with what felt like a gallon of white goo.

But it wasn't a gallon, probably only a shot glass worth of fake semen.

Now, while she slept her sated sleep, he was awake, lying in a wet spot, and experiencing what women have experienced ever since men had discovered they could, through the simple act of sex, own women.

He hadn't cum because, like a man, she was too inconsiderate to attend to his needs.

He was horny, and he wanted to jack off, but he couldn't. Even if he could have stroked his hog, he wouldn't have, for fear she might wake up and be displeased.

He couldn't even leave the room for a quick masturbation session. Not only might she sense him leaving the bed and pull him back, but he had the chastity tube on.

So he lay in the puddle of her goo and wondered where was the glory?

And the answer was in the pounding heart in his chest.

Denied, he wanted sex more and more.

Then he smiled. Breakfast was coming, and that would provide him with what he needed. Maybe not as good as a cum, but maybe better.

Feeling the warm squish of cum under him, he closed his eyes and drifted off to sleep.

END

Full Length Books from Gropper Press

Rick Boston and his beautiful wife, Jamey, move to Stepforth Valley, where Rick is offered a job at a high tech cosmetics company. The House of Chimera is planning on releasing a male cosmetics line, and Rick is their first test subject. Now Rick is changing. The House of Chimera has a deep, dark secret, and Rick is just one more step on the path to world domination!

The Stepforth Husband

Feminized by Two Sisters!

Cheater gets the ultimate comeuppance!

Grace Mansfield

A Note from the Author!

I've said it before and I'll say it again. Men shouldn't cheat. Not if they know what's good for them.

Gary is a bit snippy with his wife. That's because he's got a nasty secret.

But now the secret is out, and Gary is about to learn what all men know, or should know.

A man should never mess with a pissed off woman.

And he really, *really* shouldn't mess with two pissed off women!

STAY HORNY!
Gracie

Part One

Judy put in the security camera for protection. She had heard of women getting beaten up, and worse, and wanted to protect herself. She called up Foster's Security Service and ordered their best cameras. She had them put in the upper corners of the room she was using.

The cameras were nothing more than specks above the ceiling molding, and showed all of the room. No hiding behind the sofa, no keeping a face hidden, unless one wore a mask, and if they wore a mask she had a gun stuck under the mattress, and she always had her hand on the gun for the first minutes of meeting with Johns. If they proved out she simply shoved the gun between the mattress and got down to business.

Never had a problem. Not a one. Until the night Gary called.

On a Tuesday night Gary was feeling restless. He worked long hours, and he had a sex drive, and Ann didn't.

Ann was his wife, and she tended to be a little irritated with him lately.

She didn't mind that he worked late, or had to go back to the office, she knew it was rough running your own business. What she cared about was his attitude.

On that Tuesday night they had a light dinner and were settled in for the night. Well, she was. He wasn't.

"Would you like to watch some TV?" she asked.

"Nah," he said, and didn't even look at her. He was looking at his iPhone.

A few minutes passed. "How about if I make a cake? I could make a chocolate chip angel food cake. I know you love them."

He frowned. "Nah."

She sighed. He was a hard man to please.

Gary stared at his phone. He was looking at the stock market, and he shouldn't have been frowning. Stocks were up, big time, and he was making money just by sitting on his ass.

But he couldn't help it. He was horny.

"Did you know the Carson's are taking a vacation?"

"Um." Damn it. He wished she'd shut up.

He was horny because his prime girlfriend, a hooker named Cindy, was out of business. He had called her to make a date, but she was no longer working. Her roommate had caught an STD and she had decided there was too much risk in the hooker business.

Which left Gary high and dry.

Damn bitch hadn't even given him a recommendation.

What had it been, two weeks since he had gotten a little relief?

"Joanie said they wanted to rekindle their marriage. Isn't that wonderful?"

He shrugged, his eyes twitching in irritation. I guess."

He left the stock market and went to his contacts. John, at the office had recommended a girl. He hadn't checked her out, she was new in town, but…damn he was randy as a goat with a boner.

"Do you ever think about that? Us talking a little vacation?"

He wasn't listening. He was cogitating over taking a chance with a new girl. Making up his mind he sent a text.

"Are you available tonight? John Winston gave me your number."

He lazed back in his recliner and stared out the blackened picture window. Dark night. Clouds overhead. No sign of the stars. He wondered if he'd get an answer.

"What do you think, honey? Would you like to take a small vacation? Rekindle that old flame?"

Ann smiled hopefully. She couldn't figure out why Gary was so grumpy lately. She thought he was making good money, he should be happy. And she offered him sex night after night, but he never seemed to be interested.

He looked at her and sighed, and considered what to say.

Nah. I'm tired of the same old same old. I want something fresh and juicy.

Man, she'd hit the roof if he said that. When did marriage get to be such a drag?

Heck, he knew she was a good looking babe. Great set of tits, beautiful face, but…he just didn't feel like it anymore. At least, not with her. "Do you, honey?"

Ding!

He grabbed his phone, he had been rescued. He was tired of making excuses to that cow. He held up a finger to her and spoke into the phone.

"Hello?"

"I got your text." Her voice was soft and sultry. Gentle, yet filled with a wry humor. The honey smoothness of her voice made his dinger dong.

"I see," he tried to sound like he was talking business, even turned away from Ann.

"My prices are $300 an hour. $1000 for a night."

"I understand. And when are you available?"

"Tonight."

God. She sounded beautiful. "Very well."

"Would you like the address?"

"Certainly."

He was on his feet now, striding back and forth, putting on the act.

Ann watched him and frowned. Not another late night meeting! She really wanted to have sex. She wanted the man who had wooed her. She wanted their relationship to heat up again.

"413 Edwards. Hotel Edwards. Room 525. Is nine o'clock okay?"

"Yes." His penis was starting to rage and he turned his body so Ann couldn't see the throbbing bump in his pants.

The woman hung up.

Gary stayed on the phone, said 'uh huh' a couple of times, then stated, "I'm sorry you have to leave town so soon. Can we meet tonight?"

Ann felt her heart sink.

"Uh huh. Okay then. I'll be over within a half. Oh, I'm sure we can hammer out the details. No, it's me thanking you. Okay."

He hung up and looked at Ann.

Ann's face was a careful mask. She didn't want to show the

disappointment she felt.

"I'm sorry, honey, but this is important. Big client, big contract."

"I understand. What time will you come home?" Hoping he would be back fast enough so they could get together.

"It might be a while. Don't wait up for me."

"All right."

He went to the foyer and took out a jacket. He went into his office and picked up a laptop. Had to make it look good. He went back to the front door and Ann was waiting.

"Gary? Are we all right?"

Fuck! "Of course we are!" he forced the smile onto his face, tamped down his irritation. *Did she have to pull this shit now?*

"Well, okay."

He gave her a quick kiss, smiled, and headed out the door.

Ann went into the kitchen, poured a glass of water and watched him back his Maserati into the street.

He was handsome, a good provider. So why did she have this unsettled feeling?

She sighed, felt alone, and decided to head for the bedroom a little early. She could at least get out the vibrator. It was a poor excuse for a man, but...but if that was all she had...

Gary drove over the speed limit. He wasn't scared of getting a ticket. He knew most of the cops in town, and they all knew him. He bought tickets to the Police Man's Ball. He contributed to charities. He was close friends with the mayor.

Edwards Street was on the far side of town, and he cut over to the freeway, zipped for a few miles, then cut back into hotel row.

There it was, Hotel Edwards, a six story building that took up a block. A small block, but still a block.

He cruised up to the front, then pulled into the horseshoe. A young fellow in a cheap suit came out and gave him a ticket and drove his car off.

He strode into the hotel.

A couple of people recognized him, and he waved. They knew him because this was a popular hotel for men.

The lobby was clean, the spittoons shined, and he stepped onto the elevator and pressed a button.

And a fat lady dressed in pink, with a miniature poodle dyed in pink, managed to squeeze her bulk through the closing doors.

He could felt the elevator dip a couple of inches as her feet, squashed in her high heels, stepped onto the elevator.

He smiled, and groaned inside. There oughta be a law! There was a weight limit on the elevator!

She smiled back at him and pressed a button. Five. Damn. The same floor as him.

The elevator, under her weight, seemed to take forever. He swore he could hear the gears grinding in the basement. Finally, the doors opened.

He stepped back and motioned for her to pass, and she did with a cheery smile. He pressed six.

He went up, he went down, and when the doors opened there was no sign of the weight challenged lady.

He smiled as he walked down the hallway. An image flashed into his mind. He opens the door to 525 and she's there, wearing a tutu. Or maybe a peignoir designed for a woman two hundred pounds lighter.

He snickered as he imagined her bulging out of the seams. Hah!

He walked to 525 and looked up and down the corridor.

Nobody.

He tapped on the door.

He heard feet, he knew the woman was probably looking through the peephole at him, but he was turned, making sure nobody popped out into the hallway. The last thing he needed was somebody recognizing him.

The door latch clicked and the door pulled back an inch. "Come in," came the sultry voice.

He pushed the door open slowly, wanted to make sure there wasn't a pimp waiting to brain him and steal his expensive clothes. That had never happened to him, but one of his friends said it had happened to him, so he was careful.

The woman was walking away from him, her back was to him, and she seemed to be in a hurry. He didn't know that she was just trying to get back to the corner of the bed so she could have a hand near her gun.

He turned and closed the door. He locked it, and heard the bed springs as she settled down.

He turned and stepped into the light.

The woman looked at him from the corner of the bed.

His first glimpse was that she was perfect. She had an hourglass body, more curves than a raceway, and a face that was…was…

She stared at him, a smile frozen on her face. No…no! It couldn't—

"Judy?"

"Gary?"

"Oh, fuck!"

She was back on her feet, and they faced each other.

"You aren't…"

"That was you on the phone?"

"You're turning tricks?" And he started to laugh.

Judy's face turned red and she glared at him.

"Laugh, clown, but you're the one that's buying."

Gary's face froze instantly. Oh shit.

Judy was Ann's sister.

She was as good looking as Ann, but she had never had much respect for Gary. And now, for him to find out that she was selling her quim to passersby…he realized what a precarious position he was in. His heart was suddenly sinking down, down, through his belly and right into his shoes.

"But…I didn't mean…"

"I know what you meant."

"Well, I'll be going."

"The fuck you will! You stand right there while I think this through."

"There's nothing to think about. I made a mistake, and…let's forget about it."

A slow smile crept across her face. It was not a pleasant smile.

"So you're stepping out on my sister. I'm sure she doesn't know."

"You're not going to tell her," he blustered. He didn't feel very confident.

"I might. That all sort of depends."

"I'm out of here."

"You leave and I'll send…I'll tell her."

She had almost let him know that she was getting all this on video, but she had caught herself in time.

"Well, what do you want?"

She felt herself growing more powerful by the second. The look on his face. He was scared, and the more scared he got the more powerful she felt. She wasn't going to let that power go to waste.

She shrugged her peignoir off and stood revealed. She wore a black half bra, her tits showing over the lip, a thong, a garter with sheer nylons, and high heels.

Her lips were red and her eyes made up.

She knew that whatever happened, she could only face one way. She could delete one camera, but not both. Or, wait, she could do some editing, and—

"What are you doing?"

Good. She could hear his fright. It sounded like his voice was higher pitched.

"You're paying for it, so I thought you should see what you're getting."

"I'm not going to fuck you!"

"You're right. This is more of what you're missing out on."

He was staring at her nipples, and he couldn't help himself. He licked his lips.

Yet, he tried, "You should be worried that I'll tell your sister what you're doing."

"As if I give a shit what my sister thinks."

Damn. She made a point there. She never seemed to care what anybody thought.

He remembered flirting with her once at a Christmas party. She had shot him down, hard, and laughed at him ever since.

No. This bitch didn't show him any respect.

"Well, I'm leaving."

"Not until you get down on your knees and eat my pussy."

"What?"

"You heard me. Now get on your knees and come get some."

Keeping her face pointed away from the camera behind her, she pulled the thin patch of material to one side.

He stared at her pussy, and perspired, and his cock actually dripped.

Damn! She had a fine body, but he wasn't going to fuck it!

Of course he was't. She had already made that plain.

But, to eat her out?

He started to tremble. He wanted to get his face down there and have a little clam chowder. Sister-in-law or not, that was mighty a fine looking vag.

And those tits…

And those red, curvy lips.

She moved to the bottom of the bed and faced him. She sat down on the bed and leaned back.

It crossed his mind: push her, leap on her, do her.

But he knew she would fight. No. He wasn't going to get any. Nothing but…a little kissing of her lower lips.

She was waiting. She could see him crumbling. She could see the fear in his eyes that she might tell Ann, and she could see the throbbing in his pants, the pounding of his heart, the way he was gulping and swallowing.

As the seconds passed he felt like he was moving back out of his head. Watching his body fold, his knees thud on the floor. Then he watched himself place his hands on her knees and lean forward.

She sighed and grabbed the back of his head.

He watched her labia, glistening with juices, half spread from her pulling her thong out of the way.

Then he touched her flesh. His tongue was extended and sliding along the inside of her labia, tasting the moist sweetness.

She was shaved, her clitoris was a little mountain at the top of her slit, he was drowning in sensation. He couldn't stop himself.

He licked, and gobbled, and ate, and chewed, and he could feel her getting tense.

Judy had a hard time keeping her face away from the camera. Her pussy was on fire. She couldn't breath. And then…and then…

Gary was on his feet. He wiped his face with his arm. The smell of her was strong, and instead of getting it off his face, he got it onto his jacket.

God, he loved that smell.

In his pants his penis was thrusting in an effort to cum.

But she was done, and she had no intention of letting him cum.

"If you squirt I'll definitely tell Ann."

"I'm leaving."

"Get the fuck out."

So he did.

Behind him, laying on the bed, totally relaxed, her pussy spent, Judy laid back and sighed.

God, that was good. And she knew that wasn't the end of it. Not by a long shot.

Then, a sudden burst of energy, she leaped to her feet. She kept her laptop in the closet, and she wanted to see what she had captured. Shortly she was seated at the little writing desk in the room and editing like mad.

On the elevator Gary wiped his jacket sleeve against the body of his jacket.

Damn. Seemed like her smell was just spreading.

His face smelled of her.

He was going to have to stop at the office and clean himself off.

Well, that was okay. He was going to be home early, and he could get a little relief from Ann. Super horny now, he had to get relief, even if it was from his wife.

Suddenly chuckling, thinking how clever he was, he had gotten to eat that bitch out and get away with it, and there was no way she was going to tell Ann anything. Not after laying down and spreading for him. Sure, it was just oral sex, but it was sex.

He gave a laugh. Now he was going to go home and fuck his wife, Gary headed through the lobby. Now grinning, he handed his ticket to the valet and waited for his car to be brought around.

Gary was whistling softly as he climbed out of the car and headed into the house. The lights were on, and he had a boner that wouldn't quit.

He stepped into the foyer and closed the door and locked it. "Ann?" he called.

No answer, and he frowned. Where was that bitch?

He checked in the living room and the kitchen. Nope.

Now walking softer, having the absurd notion that he was going to catch her in flagrante. It was ridiculous, but that was the way his mind, a cheater's mind, worked.

He found her in the bedroom. The lights were off and she was breathing softly. Damn! She had gone to bed early! And he really wanted a little!

He stood and stared at the lump on the bed, imagined her curvy bed writhing under him, his penis spitting into her. But he knew she'd be angry if he woke her up.

Standing there, Judy's juices on his face, he didn't smell the thick smell of sex in the room.

He didn't know that Judy had just finished a marathon session of vibratory delight. He didn't know her pussy was raw from excessive use. He didn't know she was awake, faking sleep, praying that he wouldn't wake her. Man, she was all sexed out.

Finally, he turned and headed back out to the kitchen.

In the kitchen he poured himself a shot and downed it. Then a second one.

He saw no correlation between coming back from sex outside the marriage and wanting a drink. He didn't understand the correlation of between guilt and breaking his marriage vows.

He was just thirsty and wanted a shot.

Finally, he went into the guest bathroom and stroked himself to an orgasm. It wasn't satisfying, but at least he got rid of his juices.

The next few days were tense. But then the last few months had been tense.

A man has two ways of acting when he is cheating. One is to be overly nice, to want to make amends for what he has done on some level. The other is to treat his wife life crap, blame her for his infidelities.

Gary chose the latter. She wasn't putting out enough. It was her fault he was always horny. He found little faults with the things she did, the way she acted. All of which was beating down on Ann, making her feel like crap.

If the man is kind and sweet, the woman usually doesn't figure it out. But if the man is a mini-beast she has two ways of reacting. One, to stand up and fight back. To confront the man and treat him like shit right back. Or, two, to wonder what she had done. To assume the blame because, darn it, she loves him too much.

Ann was number two. She was constantly asking herself what she had done. She cooked his favorite dinners, she tip toed around him, she wanted to know what she had done so she could correct her behavior.

The result of this was more and more tension, less and less of the loving companionship that is core to a marriage.

It is difficult to estimate how long this situation would have lasted. It might have gone on for years before Ann had finally seen the light, had realized, in some manner, that it wasn't her.

It didn't go on for years.

"Oh, my God! Gary! You won't believe what happened!"

Gary was barely in the door. It had been a light day, he hadn't had any escort, he still hadn't found one he trusted, and that experience with Judy…he shivered.

"What?"

Her excitement had him a bit mystified, and quite curious. She was just bubbling with energy and acted like she had a huge secret.

She did.

"Honey, let me pour you a drink, you're going to need one."

Truly puzzled, he followed her into the kitchen. She poured him some Whistlepig, asked him if he wanted Coke, and he did.

She finished the drink and placed it on the table. She poured her own, easy on the bourbon heavy on the Coke, and sat down opposite him.

She was energized like he had never seen her, and there was a sexiness here that made him aware of his penis. Her face was flushed and she was so alive.

"Well, you know my sister, Judy…"

Gary's mind froze. He kept his eyes moving, he gulped his drink, he kept breathing, but the panic was exploding through his body.

"We've been a little cool the last couple of years, but she called me up, out of the blue, and she wanted to talk. And, man, she had some stuff to say!"

Gary's mind unfroze and raced, but everywhere it went was a cul de sac, or led to a cliff, or just went into an endless loop de loops.

Had Judy blown the whistle? No. Or Ann wouldn't be so excited. This was not a woman reproaching him for cheating. This was a woman truly excited about something.

But it was about Judy! And all Gary could think about was how he had had his face planted in Judy's delicious pussy. He had even jacked off to it a few times since then. But…what…

Ann was going on, her eyes sparkling, fully alive.

"She told me that she'd been having a rough time, and that she had, get this, been having affairs with men! Can you believe it? She's always been a little loose, but she has been going out and screwing men, and, get this…charging them for it!"

Gary tried to speak, but his throat wasn't working right. He cleared it and injected, "Maybe you shouldn't be telling me this."

"Oh, no! She said no secrets. She said she was implementing some sort of 12 step plan for sex, be honest with everybody. She even said, explicitly, 'you can even tall Gary about it.' She wants to get over the shame, she wants to come clean with the world. Isn't that amazing?"

"Uh, wow. Uh, yeah." He thought about telling Ann that he didn't want to hear anymore, but there was a morbid fascination. Judy hadn't told her about him, so what was she doing?

That it had to do with him he knew. There was absolutely no reason for telling this to Ann, except to…to get back at him.

"She said she had been going to the Edwards Hotel. The same one you use for your meetings! And she charged $300 an hour. She said men even paid her as much as $1000 a night! Can you believe it?"

His hand was shaking and he put it in his lap, made a fist, tried to get rid of the shakes.

"She might have been in a room fucking some stranger while you were meeting with one of your clients! What are the odds?"

Finally, Gary forced himself to speak. "I don't believe it!" He put the proper spin on his voice, came across as innocent and amazed and stunned. "I always thought she was okay looking, but men would actually pay her that much?"

Heart pounding as he covered his lies with truth. He knew what Judy charged.

"I know. It's unbelievable. And she said the men were all married! That's what gets me. How could anybody cheat on their wife! Thank goodness we have a rock solid marriage."

"Yes. Thank goodness." He kept the tremble out of his voice, but not out of his chest. He didn't know how much more of this he could stand. He needed to get away, to think about this, maybe to…yes…to have another drink.

He pushed his glass across the table and gave a wavery smile.

Ann didn't appear to notice the insubstantiality of his smile and picked up the glass. As she made his drink she continued. "Anyway, we talked for a long time. She really poured her heart out, along with some very salacious details. I ended up inviting her over for dinner this Friday. I hope she still feels like talking. I really want to hear all about this. Don't you?"

"Oh, yeah!" He tilted his glass and gulped. The liquor pouring down his throat didn't calm him.

The next couple of days were nervous ones for Gary, to say the least.

Now he was caught, terrified of being revealed, and he started getting a little jumpy.

It didn't help that Ann kept talking about it. And he couldn't tell her to shut up, he couldn't even hint to her that he had heard enough. He didn't want to act untoward in any manner. So he listened, and he worried, and Friday ground down on him.

And, like a hammer descends on a nail, be it in slow motion, it was Friday. Then he was done with work and had to go home.

"Dress nice," Ann said. "I mean, casual is okay, but…we want her to be relaxed."

"No problem," he answered, his nerves officially shot.

"And be polite. Don't be snippy to her. She's unburdening her heart. She's turning over a new leaf. We've got to be there for her.

Ding dong!

Gary almost crapped, he was so wound up.

"Get the door, honey," Ann called from the kitchen. "I'm making the drinks!"

Feeling like a stranger in his own body, Gary gripped the knob, pulled, and the door swung back.

Judy was looking good. She was wearing a tight dress with a cross over vee to present her cleavage. Her dress was short, but not too short, but short enough to show her spectacular legs.

Gary was immediately reminded of how she had pulled his head into her pussy, how she had clutched him and even pounded on his back before shivering in a massive orgasm.

He put his hands to his lips unconsciously, reminded himself of her taste, of the soft, pink flesh that had kissed his mouth back.

She grinned, and he saw the look in her eyes. The humor. The 'gotcha' in her expression. Oh, fuck. She was here for blood!

"Hello, Gary, dear."

She stepped into the foyer and gripped his right arm with her left hand. With the other hand she slipped something into his jacket pocket.

What the fuck?

She touched her cheek to his. "Better look at it alone," she whispered.

"So good to see you!"

Perfect timing, Ann stepped out of the kitchen with three glasses clutched in her hands. "Here go, kiddies!"

Gary grabbed two of the glasses and handed one to Judy.

“Oh, thank you! I need this. After what I’ve been through.”

“Oh, you poor dear! Come into the living room and we can talk about it. Dinner’s cooking, and…come on.”

Ann led Judy into the living room.

Gary tried to weasel out. “I should check my email.”

“No,” Ann shot him a look. “We’re Judy’s support group. You can check your mail later.”

Gary nodded. He had no choice, even though whatever Ann had put in his pocket was all he could think about. It felt like it might be a disk, but…well, crap. He followed the girls into the living room.

They sat on the wrap around couch, able to see each other, Judy between them.

They all sipped, and talked lightly, Ann very encouragingly, and the conversation went from mild to pithy in a matter of minutes.

“So how did you get started?” asked Ann.

“A man flirted with me, I was a little high, and he asked how much. I thought he was kidding, and I threw out a figure. He said, ‘sure,’ and that was my first one.”

“What was it like?”

“It was incredible. It was stolen cookies. I didn’t know he was married, but he actually called out his wife’s name in the middle of it. Later I asked him and he admitted it.”

“Honey!” Ann glared at Gary. “Can you believe it? Oh, that man!”

“It’s not all the man’s fault,” Judy murmured. “Sure, there are some weak men, all they want is the sex. horny, little bastards, but…they’re out of control. But it’s the ones that are strong and take charge that got to me. Every woman wants a strong men, and these men…they were like predators.”

Gary felt like she was talking directly to him, calling him names, naming him out.

“Oh, that’s terrible!”

“At first it wasn’t, then, somewhere along the line, it was. Somewhere along the line I realized that I wasn’t getting love, I was getting a loaner, and a pretty badly beat up one. Even when they were nice there was an attitude. They looked down on me, treated me like I was just an object, and…and I began to feel that I was being used, and that not even $300 an hour was worth it."

"$300 an hour!" Ann's eyes were wide.

"Oh, yes. And a thousand for a night. But most of them just wanted to bend me over, stick their dick in me and slap my ass."

"Oh, my God!"

But while Ann was shocked, Gary was excited. This was what he did! This was becoming a play by play on how he acted, what he did, and now, to actually hear of her performing sex acts, and remembering how he had been face deep between her legs…his pecker was jumping around in his pants like a Mexican jumping bean on steroids!

"What…what kind of sex did these men want? I mean…I don't…"

"It's okay," murmured Judy, brushing at her eye with a hankie. "It's helping me to get it off my chest."

Gary stared at her chest. He was prisoner to his words, and Judy glanced at him and there was a look in her eyes. Malicious victory. Gary forced his eyes up.

"Men mostly liked it two ways. They either wanted to lay on me, they'd suck my tits and finger bang me, then they'd jam their cock into me. It was almost like they were trying to hurt me."

"They were so disgusted with themselves they took it out on you," Ann blurted.

"I think so. Then there were the ones who just wanted me to bend over. I even had to take it…take it…"

"Up the ass?" Gary surprised himself with his exclamation. But he was getting so excited, and she had been hemming and hawing and he wanted to get on with it!

"Gary!"

"No, it's okay. I've got to face it." Judy looked directly at Gary. "Yes, there were men who got off on fucking my asshole. The first time it was an accident, some guy aimed for my pussy, but he was drunk and his penis slipped right into my rectum. It hurt, but then it didn't, and he was just sawing away, and…and I realized it felt pretty good. The…I found myself pushing back, trying to get more."

"Oh, you poor dear."

"It's okay. I'm over it now. but…it wasn't just those two positions, the missionary and the doggy. It was some weird stuff every once in a while. I had one guy," she lowered her voice and looked back and forth between them, "and all he wanted to do was eat me. Perform cunnilingus. He didn't want to screw me. He didn't want to kiss or make out or fuck. He just wanted to lay between my legs and…and eat my pussy. I couldn't believe it. That guy was so weird, and…and I wonder how some men can be so sick!"

"Oh, gosh," Ann breathed.

Gary was skewered. His own guilt was being shoved right through his psyche. His face was turning red and he wanted to get out of there.

"Anyway, in the end that sicko couldn't even cum. I don't think he could. He was just a crazy pervert, and…and…"

Judy began to cry.

Ann patted her back. "It's okay. It's all over now. You're among friends."

Eventually Judy stopped crying, but the looks she kept giving Gary all night long…he didn't know if he was going to cum or puke.

Part Two

The dinner had taken everything out of Gary. He was a wreck, but he was keeping it on the inside.

Judy had gone and Ann was doing the dishes.

“Well, that came off well.”

He stared at her back and suddenly hated her.

And immediately felt guilty and loved her.

He felt like he was going crazy.

For the first time in his life the thought flitted across his mind: *maybe it's me.*

But it was just a whim of a thought, like one of those flies that were too small to even track down and swat. Buzz buzz, right in front of his eyes, then gone.

“That was rough,” he spoke of Judy’s visit, but he was revealing his agitation.

Ann took it the right way and shook her head sadly. “How can men do these things.”

“It was her, too,” he protested, again double meanings colliding in his mind.

“Oh, I know. There would be no drug smuggling if there weren’t addicts, but you still have to blame everybody.”

Not much he could say to that.

She spun around, her hands suddenly wiping on her apron. “Thank God I’ve got you! Heysoos! I would hate to be in a relationship with a cheater.”

Then she was across the room and in his arms. She was hugging, and he realized how deeply her sister’s situation had affected her.

He held her and realized she was crying.

“Hey,” he said, suddenly shocked.

Suddenly feeling…bad. He didn't have enough self awareness to realize why, but he did.

"Thank God. Thank God." she murmured into his chest.

Then a long minute of just standing there. Her comfortable in his warm arms, him trying to figure out how he could get out of this.

Heck, he still had a disk to look at!

Then she suddenly chuckled, her voice echoing in his chest in a dull way. "Can you imagine me renting my body out to strangers?"

He blinked.

Then she was laughing. "Come on, big boy. You want the front door or the back. Oh, you just want to eat me? That's okay. I'm sick, too."

Then she was quiet.

Once again his mind was whirling, trying to figure her emotions out.

She had been affected, and she was making jokes to relieve the torment in her mind.

Then her hand snaked down and she felt his pants.

"Oh, my God! You're horny!"

She looked up at him, and she was smiling, but there were currents here that he dared not swim in.

"What was it that got you horny? Was it her talking about the way men took her?"

"No. Wait…no." He didn't know what to say. But he was horny. His cock was rock hard, and it didn't help that now she had her hand in his pants, was holding the shaft and gently stroking, squeezing.

Then she was kissing him.

He kissed back, but she pulled her mouth away and frowned at him.

"Are you just like other men? If you had the chance would you fuck my sister?"

"No!" And he hadn't. Not that it had been much of a chance, but…he had only eaten her.

"Why is there something in me that doesn't believe me."

"I don't know. I think you're being silly."

"Am I? Come on."

She pulled on his dingus and led him through the house.

"You haven't fucked me for a while, and now I'm wondering why. Maybe you have some hooker waiting for you somewhere."

Oh, fuck! he wailed inside.

She dragged him into the bedroom, she turned him, making him yelp with her grip on him, and pushed him over the bed. Face down. Bent. His ass, though still in trousers, up.

"Is this the way you like it?"

She stepped against him, rammed her hips against his buns.

"Is this what men want?"

She dry humped him then. He had longish hair and she knotted her fist in his hair and pushed him, pulled him, humped his rump.

"Hey!"

Then she was pulling him up, by the hair, and he went with it, pain twisting on his face, and she pushed him back over the bed, now on his back, and kissed him.

And kissed him.

Hungry, vicious, demanding.

Then she pushed off him. She stared at him, and he stared at her, and for the first time in his life he was actually a little scared of her.

She was breathing hard, and the look on her face, in her eyes…

"What's got into you?"

She stepped back and slowly took her clothes off. She unbuttoned her blouse, unzipped and dropped her skirt. She stood in panties and bra and her eyes, it was like that thousand yard stare they talk about men in combat getting.

She wiggled out of her panties, then reached for him. She grabbed him by his handle.

"Eat me, you bitch."

She spun him around, laid back on the bed and spread her legs.

He could see what was going on in her mind, how Judy's stories had excited her, but…

"I said eat my pussy. Eat me good enough and I might let you fuck me."

She did a half a sit up, leaned forward enough to grab his hair, and she pulled him down to her.

Just like that night a month ago, he was mouth deep in pussy. But now it was his wife. It was okay, and he began to chew like a demon. He licked and sucked. His hands went up to her breasts and she slapped them down.

"Just your mouth, bitch!"

Just the mouth it was. For long minutes he lost himself in the sacred portal. His penis was like a lance, touching the side of the bed as he pushed her back across the bed with his mouth.

Ann held his hair now, tangled in her claws, pulling him into her. She began lifting and smashing his face into her womanhood. After months of him ignoring him, working late, having to use the vibrator. God! This felt good!

Then, her slit pleasured enough, she pulled his hair.

"Oh!" he yelled as she yanked him to his feet and pulled him between her legs.

His penis sunk into her and she gasped. She was hanging on, pounding on his back, and the orgasms started.

Rod lay on his back. His back was bruised, and he had scratches on it. His whole body felt like it had been through a wringer. A sexual wringer.

Next to him Ann slept peacefully.

He had never been fucked like that. Sure, a little slap and tickle, but…he felt like he had been pulled through a meat grinder by his dick.

Her chest rose and fell rhythmically. Her large breasts were mountains, the nipples hard in her sleep.

Probably dreaming about how she had taken him, roughly, like he really was just a bitch.

She mumbled something, some sweet nothing.

He slid his legs out from under the covers, then was standing on the floor, and looking right at his shame.

He hadn't been able to cum! She must have squirted a dozen times, but he hadn't cum once. His dick was hard enough, it throbbed, it pulse, but…it didn't squirt.

Traitor," he chastised the rod sticking out between his legs.

And he was all the hornier for it.

He bent and picked up his jacket and felt in the pocket. There it was. He was right, it was a disk. Holding the disk, he padded across the floor. He slipped through the door and closed it softly.

He powered up the computer and stared at the disk. What the fuck. He was afraid of it. He thought it might be blackmail. And if it was…

He slid the disk into the tray and watched the screen. An icon popped up and he double tapped it.

A menu with the contents. And the contents were a single folder.

He opened the folder.

A video. Huh?

And a letter. He expected some kind of letter, but a video? He clicked on the video and it opened up, and his eyes opened wide and he almost pissed in his pants.

It was him, in room 525. He heard the first exchange between himself and Judy. His face was not red now, it was pale. This was the stuff of divorces! This was his house, his cars, his savings and stocks and…and everything, all in a leaky boat slowly sinking beneath the waves.

He watched as he stood at the foot of the bed, and saw how he couldn't identify Judy. She wore her hair different and she never really gave enough of a view to be seen.

His heart felt like it was bouncing in a bass drum in his belly as he sank to his knees and began eating.

The look on his face. Crazed. Sex crazed. And the eagerness with which he performed this act of cunnilingus. Holy fuck a moly!

He clicked the video off. He would have yanked that disk out and snapped it in two and burned it and scattered the ashes except there was a still a letter to read.

He opened the letter.

Nine PM

This Friday night.

526 at the Edwards

Or else

That was it. No signature, nothing else. Just location and time and…a threat.

Or else what?

He knew. Or else she would send the video to her sister.

His marriage would be over.

He would be broke, homeless, and all because of that…that…cunt!

He closed the letter. No need to memorize the contents, they would be burned into his psyche forever.

He took out the disk and broke it. Not that that would do any good. She would have copies, and it was probably up on the cloud. Hell, it might even be on Facebutt!

He put the pieces of the disk into the trash and stared at the computer. For the first time in a long time…he wasn't hard. Not a bit.

It was several days until Friday. Days of torture. Days of not able to do anything but think about what was going to happen?

Why did she want him to go to room 526? Why not room 525? Had she just switched rooms?

Why did she want to see him at all? She had no interest in sex, not with him. So why?

He thought about the implications and what he could do.

He could wear a disguise. He could not show up. He could knock on the door and refuse to go in. He could…nothing worked in his mind.

The truth of the matter was that he was in a trap and he couldn't even gnaw his leg off.

A day passed.

He went to the hotel and wandered through it. He scoped the various floors. He managed to walk past room 526 when a maid was cleaning it, and it was the same as room 525, just a reverse floor plan. Why 526?

Another day passed. He sat at work and chewed on his fingernails and didn't get a bit of work done.

And, one more day, and it was Friday.

He arrived home early after work, and he just hung out.

"Don't have any meetings tonight?" asked Ann.

"I have one later."

"Don't you wish your clients understood that it's a weekend? That they respected your time?"

"They're from overseas," he blithely lied. "Different clock. Limited time here."

"Oh, well. It's still too bad."

They had dinner and he was silent, thinking, worrying.

"You sure are quiet tonight. Is anything wrong?"

"No…no. Just worrying about that client."

"Well, if it was me I'd tell them to forget it."

"That's how I make my money," he observed, not really thinking.

After dinner he sat in front of the computer and just sat. He had nothing on, was just staring at his desk top and seeing the file he had read.

Nine PM

This Friday night.

526 at the Edwards

Or else

He saw it in his sleep. It was all he saw these days.

Then it was close to nine. He moved sluggishly, making his body move in spite of his reticence. He put on casual clothes that would be acceptable for work, and acceptable to a whore.

Not that a whore has standards, he thought obliquely.

"Good luck, honey," Ann smiled from behind a magazine.

He gave her a sickly grin and headed out.

Across town. The valet absconded with his car. Through the lobby. Up the elevator.

He stopped in front of room 526 and knocked on the door.

It swung back. Nobody there. WTF?

He pushed it the rest of the way and peeked inside. Nope. Nobody. Maybe the bathroom?

He stepped all the way in, his heart pounding like a rabbit in front of a wolf.

There were some clothes on the bed, it looked like she had gotten undressed, and a note. But where had she gone? What was going on?

He ignored those and looked in the bathroom. A bottle of Nair on the sink. A tube of lipstick. The circle on the bottom of the tube showed it was bright red.

WTF?

He walked back into the bedroom and looked at the note on the bed.

It was on top of what looked like a black dress and some underwear. A bra and panties and garter and nylons. A pair of high heels. A wig.

Frowning, he picked up the note.

Use the Nair. Put on the underwear and dress.

Use the lipstick. Put on the high heels. Put on the wig.

Come to 525.

If you do this I will give you all the copies of the video I have.

If you don't, they go to your wife.

He was gulping frantically. He was having a panic attack. The room rocked and rolled, and he placed his hands on the bed, gripped the covers in his fists, and tried to stop the world.

Dress up in these…these things. This was girl's stuff.

Cross the hall.

But he would get the video.

If he could do this he would be free.

If he didn't…it was all over.

What choice did he have?

What else could he do?

He couldn't call the police and plead blackmail. They would just laugh at him. He was the John, and they would figure he deserved this.

He stood for long minutes, trembling, positive that his life was over.

How long does a panic attack last?

How long does insanity last?

He straightened up, then he went into the bathroom.

He had never used Nair, but it was simple. It was a spray on, and he could reach all the hard to reach places, even the center of his back, because it was a spray.

The spray turned into a gel and started burning, so he got into the shower. He washed his hair off. Individual hairs slithered down his body and rinsed into the drain. His skin felt…electric.

He knew he was breathing, but he couldn't focus on that. All he could do was the next step.

He went into the bedroom and picked up the bra and panties. He pulled on the panties, and his cock started to wake up.

He had been so panicked that he hadn't paid any attention and his member was limp. Putting on the kinky clothes it woke up, stood out, and started pounding.

Oddly, this actually helped him concentrate.

Next step. He pulled up the garters They went over his hips easily.

He sat down and rolled the nylons up his now bare legs. His legs were pale and sort of ugly, but the slick nylon changed all that.

He. fastened the nylons, then put on the bra.

It was the bra that unnerved him the most. Something about the illusion of actually having breasts, that mark of a woman.

The cups were solid, filled with something, and it looked like he actually had a pair of tits.

The dress was stretchy, but still tight. He pulled it down over his head, wiggled into the bit of material and stared at himself in the mirror.

He was starting to look female, at least in the body.

Sure, he was a bit thick, but not that much. The lines of the dress made him look thinner.

He put on the high heels and was three inches taller. He was also awkward. He tried to walk, his ankles almost gave way, but…he could do this.

Okay. Time to…time to…the lipstick.

He had been trying to forget it, but he couldn't. How could he? You look at a woman's face and the lipstick marks her as a woman.

Now he had to mark himself.

He staggered into the bathroom and picked up the lipstick. He twisted the base, and the pillar was bright red.

He had seen his wife do this at home so many times, and…and…his cock was trying to burst through the material of the panties and dress. He was crunched down in there, and…and he looked at his lips.

Damn! this was really turning him on!

Now he wasn't having a panic attack, now he was just turned on.

He had never worn stuff like this! He had laughed at the idea of men crossdressing. But now he knew.

He knew why thy did it. He knew the feeling of his penis more erect than it had ever been. His body hotter, his psyche hornier.

Fuck!

He painted his lips, now taking his time, watching the red roll on and make his face almost totally feminine.

He wanted to cry, and he wanted to jump up and yell hosanna!

He twisted the tube and replaced the top and stood and stared at himself.

He couldn't breath. He looked like a woman. A little plain, a few masculine lines, but…a woman.

Now not thinking, he turned and went to the door.

The hallway was empty. Not a sound. Nothing but his pounding heart.

It was only a few steps to cross the hall. Awkward in his heels, but easy.

He ran on his tip toes, it was easier than trying to put his weight on his heels, and tried the doorknob.

It turned.

The door pushed back.

He stepped into the room.

It was quiet, but he could feel human presence.

She was here!

On the right was a small kitchenette. He walked down the short hallway and stepped into the room, and…froze.

Judy was sitting on the bottom of the bed, her sexy legs crossed. She was wearing a dress similar to his, but hers was filled out, fit her better.

Next to her, looking more like a twin than just a sister, was Ann. Wearing the same outfit.

They watched him, their lips pursed, their eyes sparkling with humor.

"What…" Gary began, but couldn't finish.

Judy had betrayed him. She had made him wear this stuff, then…Ann must have seen the video. His life was over.

"My. He looks sad."

"Hi, honey. I found out that you're a cheater."

"Bu…bu…"

Judy remarked, "I actually showed her the video right after I took it. She's my sister. I had to show her."

Ann: "So we concocted this plan. You see, Judy told me what men really want."

Both girls stood up, and Gary's jaw dropped. His mind went slack. His penis bounced so hard bits of pre-cum soaked into the dress.

"You…I…"

They were wearing strap ons. They each had a large penis jutting out from their junctions.

"You see, I didn't tell you guys what most men pay for. Not the fuck, or the suck, but…to be fucked."

"You…I…can't…"

"So we're going to give you what you want."

"But I don't!" he managed to blurt.

"But you do," countered Ann. "Or I'm taking the house, the cars, the savings the stocks…you won't even own your own company. I'll own it. And I can fire you, or let you work for minimum wage."

Talk about a world crashing down around his shoulders.

Yet, seeing the women with their jutting members…his penis pushed against the dress, and the women saw the wet spot where the bulge was.

They grinned. "I think he likes it."

"Doesn't matter. He's got no choice."

Ann moved forward on one side of him, Judy on the other side. They linked his arms and moved him towards the bed.

"Put your hands down on the bed, honey. Bend over and show us what you have."

He had no strength. He couldn't move, but he could be moved. Judy pushed his upper body forward and he bent.

Ann lifted his dress and pulled his panties down.

Judy kicked her heels off and stepped up on the bed. She stood in front of him and aimed her member at his face.

"Come on, baby. Show me a good time."

He felt Ann fumbling with her penis behind him, lining up on him, then…then…

He grunted as she slammed into him. His mouth opened in shock, and Judy pushed her tool into his throat.

Epilogue

Gary lay on the bed on his belly. Judy was behind him, riding his sweet buns, thrusting in and out.

His eyes were glazed, but he understood what was happening.

Ann was sitting against the head of the bed, her legs spread, his face was pressed between her thighs.

She tasted so sweet. Like honey. And so juicy.

"So here's how it's going to go, honey," she spoke cheerfully. "Judy is moving in with us. We're going to get you a pair of breasts, real implants." She looked up at her sister. "Is that an oxymoron? Real implants?"

"Real…fake…tits…yeah. Probably. She grunted between each word as she thrust deep into him.

"Anyway, we'll get you tits, and clothes and things, and you'll be our little sexpot. You can do your work at the company, then come home and we'll do you."

"Tell…him…about…chastity."

"Oh, yes. We're going to chastise you. Either that or castrate you. Do you have a preference? We certainly don't want to leave you with a big, old boner. After all, you'd probably just cheat again.

He tried to talk, but only succeeded in motor boating her pussy.

"Oh, yes, talk to me, lover!" She groaned and pulled on her nipples, and she began to cum. And cum. And cum!

END

Full Length Books from Gropper Press

MY HUSBAND'S FUNNY BREASTS

It's not so funny when
it's happening to you!

GRACE MANSFIELD

Tom Dickson was a happy camper. He lived a good life, had a beautiful wife, then he started to grow breasts, his hair grew long, and his body reshaped. Now Tom is on the way to being a woman, and he doesn't know why.

This book has forced feminization, cross dressing, hormones, gender transformation, pegging and breast growth.

My Husband's Funny Breasts

The Feminization of Jack

It felt good to be soft

Grace Mansfield

PART ONE

"Oh, no!"

"What?" Molly, my wife looked out of her closet at me.

We were getting ready for a charity auction and I was looking down at my belly.

"Look!"

My belly was protruding, I couldn't get the buttons buttoned.

"Oh, Jack," she laughed. "Did you get preggers?"

"Not funny."

"Well, just suck it up." She started giggling. What a hilarious wife, eh?

"I'm not going."

"Oh, yes. You are. And that is that."

"Well, that may be that, but this is this, and I'm not going. Tomorrow I'll start a weight loss program. Sign up for Weight Watchers, or something."

"Jack," I could almost hear her frowning in the closet. "You know I look forward to these events. They are a lot of work, and they really change lives."

I sighed and sat on the bed. "Well, you'll just have to do without. No way I am going to go looking like a fat slob." I punched my belly roll and wondered how I had gotten in this shape.

Suddenly something hit me in the face.

"Ack…what?"

I held up the item that had been thrown at me. It was a corset.

"Put that on."

"You've got to be kidding!"

"I am not. You are not going to deprive me of my night out, especially after the months of work I've been doing.

"There is no way I can get this on, even if I was willing, which I am not."

Molly came all the way out of the closet then, and she came with an angry lioness look on her face. She stomped towards me, grabbed my shirt with both hands and snarled in my face. "You will go."

Now, my wife is beautiful. She's willowy with boobs big enough to be called mountains, and she works out daily so she is strong. Her face is patrician, with a Roman nose, slender and aquiline. She is…we both looked down.

My cock had sprung up and poked her in the thigh.

We looked at each other. She laughed. "Well, I guess we know who's calling the shots."

"Just because I've got an erection it doesn't mean you can push me around!" Was my voice sounding just a little bit whiney?

"Oh, yes it does. It does!" She reached down and grabbed Mr. Happy and throttled him gently. Her voice changed pitch, became softer, instead of a lion she was now a pussy cat. Her other hand grabbed my testicles. "Honey, you like it when I talk tough to you, and you like it when I talk softly, like now."

"Urk," I gulped.

She lifted, and I went to my tip toes. I pushed down on her wrists but she had the leverage. "Now, we can do this the hard way…"

She held my balls in an iron grip and stroked my cock. Hard.

"Or we can do this the easy way."

She pushed me back and I fell back on the bed. She leaped on me and the look on her face was victorious and smirky all at the same time.

"AGH!"

She slipped over me, engulfed me, and I felt the velvet grip of her cunt suddenly strangling Mr. Happy. She placed her hands on my shoulders and pressed her weight on them.

I couldn't move. Not that I wanted to. There's few things I like more than a good fuck. In, there's nothing I like better than a good fuck. And my wife, to be blunt, is a good fuck.

I felt her muscles gripping me as she corkscrewed her hips, and the edge of her pussy turned and twisted.

"Oh, God!" I reached up and grabbed her awesome mounds. Her nipples were excited and felt rough against my palms.

She kissed me, took my lips in her teeth and pulled, sucked my tongue, fused her mouth to mine.

Well, there was no way I was going to last long with that amount of lust perched on me. I started to push my hips up and she stopped moving.

"Hey!"

She sat stride me, impaled, giving a little shiver, and she said, "You will wear that corset!"

"No!"

"Very well, have it your way." She began to quake. She is an easy cummer, always has been, and now she came quick and fast and hard. Almost manlike. No easy climb and gentle fall, but a sheer blast of white hot fever.

"Hey!" I gasped. I tried to move, but she held her weight on me, kept me immobilized. Her head dropped and her hair hung down to my face.

"Let me move! Let me get off!"

She gave a final shudder, then pushed off me. Her grin was downright evil.

She stood over me, smirking, and said, "There are those that cum to an event in a corset and get to cum, and then there are the other types of fools. No cum. Doomed to live a life of frustration."

I stared up at her. My cock was glistening with her juices. My heart was pounding. I had been on the edge, and now I was deprived.

"Honey, you can't do this."

"If you wear the corset you will look handsome, debonair, nobody will know, and I will fuck your brains out when we get home."

I was breathing hard, my cock was bouncing up and down madly. That's the thing about being deprived, being. teased and denied, it makes you want it more.

"Now, I'm going to the event, and if you were a manly man you'd suck it up and put that corset on. Or you can be a little pussy and not cum for a week. Or maybe a month. Or maybe not until the next time we have an event—what's that? Three months? Or if we skip it, and we might because of COVID, you could be talking about six months. Maybe even a year."

"I'll jack off."

"Now who's the pussy?" she slid that quip into me like a knife into butter.

Funny, she didn't mind getting herself off, but she was particular vicious at the idea of me getting myself off.

She grabbed my cock. "What's it going to be, bub? Paradise or purgatory?"

I managed to squeak out, "Paradise!"

She grinned. "I'd gloat, but it's not ladylike. Heh heh heh!" she gloated.

So I took off my shirt and stepped into a corset. Man, she loosened it up, but it was still tight. And it was hell just to get it over my bobbing cock.

"Ooh, I like this!" She kept laughing and slapping my weenie.

Finally, I was in, and now the tough part, she began to lace me up.

"God, you really have been scarfing the cookies!" She knelt on my back and pulled the strings. Slowly, slowly, and with much suffering, my waist became, well, not svelte, but better. And the weird thing, my chest swelled.

She stood me up and inspected me, and took note of the way my flesh had been pushed up. "You've got little titties." She placed her hand over my pectoral and cupped my little mound.

"Hey!"

Sproing! My cock hit her thigh.

She looked down. She looked up at me. She grinned. "If I didn't know better I'd say you liked wearing this female undergarment. You actually like having little titties."

"Hey!" but I was weak. I could hardly breath, I was being bullied, I didn't have enough force in my voice.

She grabbed my handle then and stroked it, and kissed me some more. Then she moved back an inch and spoke into my face. "We're going to have to explore this. Some panties. Maybe a bra." My cock surged and she grinned harder. "The peeny never lies."

"Stop it!" I said. Again, I didn't sound strong.

"Some nylons, and…I've got it, long red nails…" my cock gave a mighty surge… "to go with your bright, red lipstick."

Splurt! I came.

We looked down in shock. My jizm was squirting all over her hand. A lot of white coated her knuckles, dripped on the floor. My knees were weak and shaking.

"Crap," I said. "You jacked me off!"

"Jacked off, hell! You jacked yourself off…with your dirty, little mind."

"Well, now I don't have to go."

Well, she had a hold of Mr. Limpit and she lifted and snarled, "Don't mess with me, cupcake!"

Damned if I didn't have an aftershock. Not a cum, not more sperm, but a shiver that went through me, weakened my knees, unfocused my eyes.

"Holy crap!" Molly muttered. Awestruck. "Holy…holy, crap!"

We went to the event. I was in the corset already, and you couldn't see it, and, let's face it, she had a hold of my prized possession, and she threatened to rip it off.

But underneath everything I could feel this lust in her. This excitement. This drive to control and hold sway over me.

She liked having this power over me.

All night long the knowledge was in her eyes. She smirked at me, dropped sly little hints that were sexy, funny innuendos to those around us, but bombshells to my addled state.

I had, after all, cum. And just from putting on a corset. And hearing all those things she said, about putting me in a bra, making me wear make up.

And, when we danced, she tried to take control. And she even put her hand on my chest, a simply placement that was understandable between husband and wife, but electrifying to my scrunched up boob.

Was this what women felt when a man played with her breasts? Did they get that shiver of excitement from a man squeezing them? And when her palm slid across my nipple I thought I was going to swoon.

She took note of my reactions and just laughed. And did them some more.

Driving home we had a conversation. It was one of the more impactful conversations in my life.

"I'm going to feminize you a little."

"I don't think so."

"But you so obviously love it. Did you feel how hard your dick was? And you came when I talked about putting you in lipstick."

"I did not!"

"Did!"

"I was just super horny. I'd been in you, you came and I didn't. I was so fucking horny I would have exploded if…if Hillary Clinton waved her ass at me."

"Lotta ass, lotta cum," quipped Molly.

"So, no. That's it. No."

"Head over to Charley Coyote's."

"What?"

"I want a drink."

"We can have one at home."

She turned to me, leaned across the center console and touched my nipple. I shivered. "Just one, widdle, bitty dwink?"

She knows I hate baby talk. Nothing irritates me like baby talk.

"Pwease?"

"Oh, fuck. Okay."

"Excellent."

I took a turn and headed for the most popular nightspot in town, at least popular for those in the know.

We didn't say anything for a minute, then she started chuckling.

"What?"

"You are so fucking easy."

I snorted, then grinned. She was right. But wouldn't you be easy if a super sexy woman was stroking your gonads?

We pulled into the parking lot and an attendant stole my car. We walked around to the front and through the entrance. This was a Thursday, and it wasn't frantic. Just crazy. A low mumble of people, a combo on the stage whispering dirty sax songs, and the heady smell of sex.

We sauntered in and looked around. "I'll grab that table. You get me something sweet that turns me on."

I headed for the bar, and fortunately I knew the bar guys, and I was a tipper. Jose saw me coming and had my obligatory Coke High ready.

A Coke High. A fancy name for bourbon and Coke. With the good bourbon, of course.

"Something fizzy and fruity for my wife?"

"We have just thee thing." He spoke with a Mexican accent and I laughed.

"Thee? Are you practicing to swim back across the river?"

Jose was born and bred in East LA. He grinned. "Naw. Boss said I'd get more tips if I sounded like a real wetback."

We laughed and he plopped a tall, thin glass in front of me. It was pink with bubbles fizzing up like an Alka Seltzer.

"What is it?"

"Jose's surprise."

I lifted my eyebrows.

"It's called a Pink Squirrel. Creme de noyaux, creme de cacao, and cream."

"Sounds creamy."

"Give her two and you'll get lucky."

We laughed, I dropped him a twenty and said, "For you. We'll run a tab."

"I'm your bitch."

I grinned at him and walked the drinks back to where Molly was waiting for me. And I thought, 'I'm your bitch.' A simple phrase, just a Hollywood expression, but…it made me think. It made me think because I was wearing a corset and Molly had been messing with my head. Panties. Bra. Lipstick.

Long, red, bright, sexy, shiny nails.

Fuck.

I reached our table, it was a booth back in a corner, and placed the drinks down.

"Ooh, what did you get me."

"Jose's Surprise." I struggled into the booth, that damned corset made motion difficult. How did women stand the things?

She looked askance at me, with raised eyebrows over the lip of her glass, as she took a sip.

"He spermed in it."

She almost lost it. She almost spit a bit of that precious liquid out, but she managed to hold it in. A bit of choking, and a cough, but she was good.

She looked over at the bar and raised her hand.

Jose saw her and she gave him a thumbs up. Jose waved and grinned.

She sipped again and faced me. "It was your sperm, if any, but I know you just came. You're empty. Drained. So what is this delicious concoction?"

"A pink squirrel," and I explained the ingredients.

"Crap," she said, "It's better than if he did cum in it."

"You're such a potty mouth," I teased.

Then she went to work on me. I sipped my bourbon and Coke and listened, and she whispered into my ear.

"I can see you all svelte and trim…with big boobs."

I looked at her. She grabbed my chin and turned my ear back to her.

"Big boobs, and wearing a bikini. But the top is too small, it keeps slipping down. Suddenly it falls all the way off. Everybody is staring at you."

"Where are we?" I asked.

"We're at a fancy party, nothing but sexy celebrities. In fact, they're all porn stars, and they all have huge boobs. But nothing like yours. They see your exposed tits and they are all jealous. They all wish they could have your boobs. Then, we're sitting there, and a producer comes over to you. He looks at your huge boobs and wants you to be in his latest flick. The name of the flick is 'He had Woman Boobs and Knew how to Use Them!'"

"I do?"

"Shut up," she pulled my face around and put her mouth so close to my ear I could feel her warm breath. Her moving lips touched my ear, teased it.

"Later, I want to go home, but you're too drunk to drive. So I take you into a bedroom and leave you. When I'm gone three porn stars sneak into the bedroom. They have ben stalking you for your tits. They are so jealous. They want to feel them, they want to suck them. And your cock. they want to suck your cock."

Oddly, the talk of them sucking my tits was more turning on than the idea of them sucking my cock. And that would have bothered me, except that Jose's Cock High…uh, Coke High…was really working.

"The three porn stars only have skimpy, little bikinis on, and they strip them off and cuddle up to you. You wake up, but you are too drunk to move, and they begin to have their way with you. Two of them are feeling your tits. Sucking on your nipples. The third one is sucking on your cock. then you feel one of their hands, you don't know which one, grabbing your butt. She grabs it and feels it and her fingers slide into your crack. You like it. You always wondered what it would feel like to have a pussy, and the way this women is feeling your rectum, you start to understand. Then she slides a finger into you. Then two fingers. You are hot. You feel like you're going to explode. Your cock is getting a mouth job, and she is feeling your nuts, but it's the two mouths sucking on your big tits that is getting to you. You arch, you poke your butt back, she has three fingers in you, and just when you think you are about to cum…"

I was breathing hard. Jose had sent another couple of drinks over and I had sucked half of mine without even being aware of it.

"Just when you are about to cum…you hear me screaming."

I tried to move away, to look at her. This wasn't the way one of her stories was supposed to go. But she held my head firmly and kept breathing into my ear.

"I'm screaming in ecstasy, while you were unconscious I was out in the big room, and you know who was there? Jose. And he had a pink drink, a squirrel thing, and I thanked him for it by getting on my knees and gobbling him. Then he pushed me back, down on my back, and everybody watched while he mounted me. He had a big, huge, Mexican dick. Far bigger than your tiny weenie. Bigger even than all the dicks I had before I was married. So I'm screaming because my hole is getting reamed and it feels so…so…so…how you doing?"

"Fuck!" I whimpered.

Molly's throat rattled with laughter. "We're going to have so much fun."

I just shook my head and sipped my Coke High. And when I was done another one appeared. Now, I don't know, but I think the way that corset was squeezing me was ambushing my ability to intake liquor. I was light-headed from my whole body being choked, and she kept pouring booze into me, and it wasn't long before I knew I wasn't driving home.

"Don't worry about it," Molly grinned. "I'll take care of you."

I was sloshed. "That's what I'm worried about."

"And you should be. Now, drink up, bitch boy."

"What?" But I drank, and the drinks kept coming, and she kept whispering dirty things to me, and telling me how she was going to feminize me, and asking why my dick was so hard when she talked tough to me and told me how she was going to give me nails and lips and dress me up like a Barby, and the next thing you know, I…

…woke up. Oh, fuck. Double fuck. My head felt like it had been drop kicked for a goal. My belly felt like a broken washing machine, spinning around, ka chunk, ka chunk, and the door flies open and I…

…ran for the bathroom. Staggering and slipping and I was caught in something, something was tripping me, and I banged against the bathroom door and just managed to upchuck on the throne. Not in it, unfortunately, but on it, because some fool had left the lid down.

Ra-a-alph! Ra-a-alph! I spewed, splashing the place up, then figuring out what was happening and lifting the lid. Ra-a-alph!

From somewhere far away I heard Molly going 'Ew! Heysoos! In the toilet!"

…awoke. Hurting. My belly aching. My throat tasting like a frog had taken a dump in it. My head…oh, God, my head…

…awoke. And was awake. Stayed awake. Lived with the feeling of somebody tap dancing in my belly. Endured the crash of timpanis in my head. Opened my eyes.

It was noonish, according to the splash of sunlight coming in through the drapes.

I just laid there, pretending that a truck hadn't rolled over my belly and squashed my contents out all over the place. I remembered upchucking. A lot. Fortunately, the pain was more of a memory.

Finally, I rolled over, stuck my feet out, and got out of bed. I swayed. I looked down. I was naked. No damned corset. And I had a weird memory of wearing one of Molly's robes, one of those peignoir things. But I wasn't wearing one now, so it must have been a dream.

I pulled on a robe, my old, tattered one, and headed for the kitchen. Not to eat, that was where we kept the aspirin.

Molly was at the sink, sipping coffee and looking out the window. She turned when I entered the kitchen and smiled. And smiled a lot. Goofy bitch.

"Hey, baby. How you feeling?"

"Gar," I muttered. I made it to the cabinet with the medicines in it and grabbed a couple of aspirin. I tossed them down the gullet and stuck my head under the faucet. After swallowing I left my head there, just let the water run over my head. Cool water.

I straightened up.

"That good, eh?"

I faced Molly. "You let me drink that much. You bitch."

"Hey, I'm not your mother. Or am I?"

"What?"

"Nothing." She was staring at me, and she was—I could feel it—belly laughing on the inside.

"I fail to see the humor in your husband dying."

"It's not that. It's…" she snickered and waved a hand and looked down. Then she looked up, holding a smile in. "Can I get you something? A piece of bread? Hair of the dog?"

"Oh…yeah. I suppose."

She made me a Bloody Mary and I downed it, and immediately my stomach started settling.

"Okay now?"

"Better." I belched.

"Cute. Well, come on. You barfed on my clothes last night, you get to help me hang them up. I already washed them."

"I barfed, eh?"

"Tossed out your kidney and your liver, almost your gall bladder."

"Har dee har…"

She took my hand and led me to the garage. She had me hold the basket and she pulled articles of clothing out of the washer. The corset.

The peignoir. A bra. Panties.

"Crap. I really got you, didn't I?"

"No worry," she was smirking. What the fuck was so funny?

Then I had a strange memory. She wasn't there, she was back in bed, or so I assumed. And I was in the bathroom, alone, heaving all over the place. So how had I heaved on her peignoir if she wasn't there?

Confused, I just stood there, well, leaned there, against the machine, and she put her dainty underthings and stuff in it, then she pointed me towards the backyard.

I managed to walk on a sort of a line out to the clothesline. I put the basket down and started hanging things up. Pulled stuff out, shook them to get rid of some of the wrinkles, then pinned them.

I wasn't more than half done when I heard the side gate bang.

"Hey, Jack!"

I pulled my robe tight and tied the sash.

It was Tom and Jenny Hawkins. My neighbors. And a bit more. We had spent a few nights drinking crazy, and one night Jenny had sat on my lap and kissed the hell out of me, while Molly sampled Tom. Nothing but fun.

"Hi, guys. What brings you out here at the crack of dawn."

They sauntered across the lawn to me, and they were staring at me in a weird manner.

"Crack of dawn. Hmmph." Jack stifled a guffaw. My 'crack of dawn' in the middle of noon wasn't that funny.

"Had a bit too much to drink last night?" Jenny put a hand on my arm and her whole face was writhing with merriment.

"Molly told you, eh?"

What the heck was so funny?

"She said you, ah…(chuckle, chuckle) really tied one on."

"You could say that. But I paid the price."

"I guess you did," snickered Jenny.

I blinked and turned to them, gave them my full attention. "Say, what's the joke?"

They lost it. Tommy actually fell on the ground, held his belly and rolled. Jenny just kept looking at me and cackling like an egg had fallen out of her ass.

"What the fuck?" It was actually a little irritating. I mean, I like humor as much as the next guy. But if something funny was happening they should let me know, let me join in the fun.

"Oh, Jack…Jack," Jenny grabbed Tommy's hand and tried to get him off the ground, all she succeeded in doing was pulling herself down, and they writhed in a puddle, laughing hysterically at I knew not what.

"What the hell is going on?"

"Hey, Jack." I turned. Molly was there, with a big smile on her face.

Her belly was actually bouncing a little as she stifled her own laughter.

"You, too? What the fuck is so funny?"

Then all three of them were laying on the ground, laughing. I have never seen anybody laugh so hard in my life.

I stood over them, hands on hips, and for the life of me couldn't figure it out.

Jenny struggled to her feet. "Oh, Jack. I could tell you, but…but…" she looked at Molly and Tom, "you would have had to have been there." Then she was falling down again, and the others were laughing even harder.

I shook my head. I was the only sane person in a village of idiots. I hung up the clothes, and every time it looked like they were going to stop laughing…they started up again. Holding their bellies, slapping their knees, laughing like a hyena on laughing gas at a joke convention.

Numbnuts. That's what they all were. A bunch of numbnuts.

I finished hanging the clothes and walked back into the house.

Numbnuts.

I went into the kitchen. There were a couple of dishes in the sink and I did them, and watched my wife friends through the window.

They were still laughing, but they were sitting, cross legged, and talking, too.

What the hell was going on?

Finished with the dishes I went in and sat down in the living room. I turned on the big screen and caught the tail end of a game. I was sitting, leaning forward, actually thinking about some lunch, when Molly came in.

"Well, are you over it?"

"I guess," but she wasn't. She snuffled down a throaty chuckle.

"You could at least let me in on it."

"I could, I suppose. But when there's a major gotcha in the works one doesn't mess with it. One lets it play out."

"So you're playing a practical joke on me?"

She nodded, and held in her laughter.

"It's funny right now?"

She nodded, her lips clamped together. Then she actually walked out of the room and started laughing.

Now, I wasn't feeling all that chipper, and I was confused, and I followed her down the hallway, into the bedroom.

"Honey, fun is fun, but you really need to let me in on the joke."

Her face was writhing, parts of it wiggling, as she tried not to laugh. She said, "Okay, hmph…um…okay. I'll tell you, but you have to do something for me."

"What?"

"Walk into the backyard naked, put on the peignoir, and come back in."

"That's it?"

"Um hmm." She put her hand on her hip and blinked to keep herself contained.

"Okay. I can do that."

"And you have to do it immediately after I tell you."

"Okay," I shrugged. What was so hard about that. "So what's the joke?"

"Go brush your teeth."

Oh, crap. I had something in my teeth, and they were all laughing at me, looking like a hayseed bumpkin or something.

I rubbed my teeth with a finger, which made Molly spurt out a squeak of hilarity, then walked into the bathroom. I looked down at the sink, was glad she had cleaned the puke off everything, grabbed my toothbrush and the toothpaste, started to squeeze out a dollop, and looked up…up…oh FUCK!

I grabbed my mouth! I actually gave a little yelp.

PART TWO

I stared at myself in the mirror. I had a fat belly and the robe had come open a little bit to expose it. My cock, damned traitor, was springing up. My lips were bright and shiny and…red.

Red. Like a sunburned fire engine. Like the color of a red mustang. Like a tomato that's embarrassed.

My hand now shaking I reached up and touched my lips. It wasn't like lipstick, it was like the color of my skin had actually been changed. And my lips actually felt a little…plumper. Maybe it was just the bright red standing out more, but my lips, now that I wasn't focused on my hangover but on my face, felt bigger. Fatter.

Like a real woman's lips.

"Oh…" I said.

"I didn't use lipstick. I used lipstain." Molly was leaning against the door jamb, her lips trembling with laughter. "Good lipstain. Guaranteed for a week. A couple of days from now they'll get a little faded, but we can use a bit of gloss and they'll pop right up.

I turned to her, aghast, my eyes wide. "I can't…you…I…"

"Now go put on your peignoir. And give me that robe. No male clothes for a week."

"But…I…work…"

"I talked to Tom at the event and told him you wanted to take a week off. And, buddy, this week is mine."

"But…but…"

"So give me that robe…" she stepped forward and grabbed my robe and started working it off me. "…and go out in the back yard, naked, like you promised, and put on that peignoir."

"I don't…you can't…"

She pushed me down the hallway.

To tell the truth, I would have welched. I wouldn't have gone out in the back yard, even though Tom and Jenny had already seen me, except that Tom and Jenny were already in the house. About the time we reached the kitchen I was starting to dig in my heels, and they were sitting at the kitchen table. Waiting for me.

"Hey, Jack," Jenny smirked.

Oh, God. My skin was flaming. It had to be the color of my lips.

"Good look, Jack," offered Tom. "Very sexy."

And I just sort of gave up. I stumbled past them, headed out the door to the back yard. Not really seeing much, just glimpses of the lawn, the surrounding bushes, the peignoir hanging from the line.

My cock was hard through all this. It had sprung up, I realized, when I had seen my face in the mirror, and it didn't seem to want to go down.

I reached the peignoir and stood, facing it, gasping for breath like I was having a heart attack. And, who knows, maybe I was.

Molly was suddenly standing next to me, and I realized I had been standing there for a while. My mind had gone into overload and literally stopped working. I was like a moose that had been bashed on the head by a wrecking ball.

"Jack?"

I turned my head and gazed at her. Oh, yeah. My wife. I was married. What was happening to me? Oh, yeah. My face. My lips. She had…she had…

"Are you all right?"

I managed to gulp and give a slow nod.

"Then put on the peignoir and let's go inside."

I nodded again. Gulped. Was aware that I had a siren's lips. Was aware of my lips. I reached out and took the peignoir down. It was dry. I must have just been standing there for a long time.

Molly helped me into it. I was like a five year old being helped into his clothes for his first day at school.

She hooked her arm in mine and walked me back to the house.

Inside the house Tom and Jenny had made drinks.

Drinks. That's what I needed. A lot of drinks.

Forgotten was my hangover. Forgotten was my roiling belly and my aching head. I just needed a drink. I picked a glass off the table and drank the whole thing.

They all stared at me. Tom started to say something, but Jenny nudged him and shook her head.

"Let's all have breakfast," announced Molly.

"Uh, yeah," said Tom.

"Okay," Jenny offered brightly.

I just stood there with my hands on the table and my head down. Breathing. My mind slowly, ever so slowly, coming back to life.

I picked up a second drink, I don't know whose it was, but it was bourbon and Coke, and slugged it down.

Again, Tom looked about to speak, but Molly said, "It's okay. He just needs to figure it out."

"Yeah," I said. "Figure it out." I looked up at the three. They were still smiling, but they were a bit nervous. Apparently they hadn't thought through to the reaction I was having.

I wasn't laughing.

I said to Jenny. "Scoot over."

Jenny slid to the side and I moved in next to her. She was dressed, I was in a peignoir, my hard cock visible through the glass table top.

I looked at Tom, who was across from me. "Hi, Tom."

He blinked, I sounded strange, but he said, "Hi, Jack."

"Hi, Jack," I mused. "I've been hijacked. At least my lips have." I grabbed a third drink. It looked like Tom had sipped from it, but I didn't care.

Tears started to come down my cheeks. I put the empty glass down. Yes, I was crying. Then I had my face down on the table and was sobbing.

Molly, Jenny and Tom were very silent now.

I cried for about five minutes. Then I stopped. Oddly, it was like a light switch being clicked. I suddenly just stopped. I looked at my three friends. They had very worried looks on their faces. I said, "Well, it looks like you got me."

I sniffed a couple of times, then looked at Molly. "Waffles. Lots of butter and syrup. I need something sweet."

Molly stood there.

And, the really odd thing, the world was crystal clear to me at that point. Every color was brighter, filled with life. The lines of the objects of the world were so sharp with clarity. I could even see the motes in the air. Life was, in a way, golden.

"Molly?" I asked, my hyper senses kicking into gear.

"Yes. Right away."

Tom tried, "Jack, we're sorry. We were just having a joke…"

I waved my hand. "And it is funny. A year from now I will be laughing hysterically, and I will always remember this massive 'gotcha.' Right now, I'm okay. I'm just coming to grips with everything."

Jenny blurted. "It's Molly's fault."

Molly spun and stared at her friend.

Jenny: "I'm sorry, but I can't…I didn't know this was going to happen like this."

Again, I waved my hand. "It's fine. Molly is the architect. You guys are just the appreciative audience. I get that."

"I'm sorry, Molly. I shouldn't have said that. I'm just…"

"Scared. Worried. Don't want me to hurt."

"Yes."

"It's okay, babe," I said to Molly. "Jenny's fine. She didn't mean anything. Now get my waffles."

Everybody was blinking and awkward, but Molly managed to turn and attend to the waffles. We had a four slot toaster and she loaded it up, put the butter and a big bottle of Aunt Jemima on the table.

Nobody was talking. Everybody was weird. So I said, "So, Tom, how's work."

It was non sequitur. It was the surrealistic moment. It was four people in a lifeboat and somebody says, 'I think I'll paddle with a sieve."

Then we were laughing. All of us. In hysterics. Couldn't stop laughing for the life of me, of any of us. Tom pounded the table so hard I thought it would break. Jenny put her hands on the sides of her face and roared. Molly held herself up with one hand on the counter, her other hand was against her face. And I…I couldn't stop.

None of us could stop.

For long minutes we laughed, and every time we slowed down we would trade a glance, or look at my lips, and start all over again.

Then the toast started burning. A little wisp of smoke rose up and Jenny pointed at it and we found that absurdly hilarious.

And we laughed and laughed and laughed.

I stood in the bathroom and stared at my lips. Red. And the rest of my face was no long as red. It had been a couple of hours, I had eaten and was over my hang over, and even my short spate of breakfast drinking. And I was actually admiring my lips.

They were full, apparently Molly had used plumper on them, long lasting plumper, and they were like a billboard in the desert of my face.

"What do you think?" Molly came and stood next to me, linked an arm in mine, and studied my face in the mirror.

"Major gotcha. Don't think I'll ever top that."

"Probably not, but I was speaking of your mouth. Pretty sexy, eh?"

"I never would have thought," I agreed. I touched them. Lipstain. Long lasting. Wouldn't come off for rubbing. And I knew she was going to keep putting on the plumper. She had 'freshened me up' with the plumper once already.

"And we're going to do the whole you."

"The whole me. Wow."

I looked at myself and not her. But then, right at that moment I was the more fascinating of us.

"Nails, make up, Jenny is actually out buying you some clothes."

"So Jenny is in on this now. How's Tom with that?"

"He's okay."

But there was something in her voice. I looked at her. That moment of clarity that had struck me before was still with me. I could read her like a book.

"Well, he's a little…he's coming to grips with the fact that she grabbed your cock."

I smiled. My teeth were extra bright for the red. "Well, it was sitting right there, under the glass."

When we had breakfasted Jenny had noted that I was hard under the glass table top, and…big. And she had asked if she could touch me. It.

I hadn't said anything. Just looked at Tom.

Molly had said, "Go ahead. He won't mind."

Tom shrugged. But he was thinking about it. His wife with her hand on another man's cock. It was something to absorb.

Now, in our bedroom a couple of hours later, Jenny asked, "Well, are you ready?"

"To be made up?"

"Yep."

"Okay."

She looked down at the sink. My cock was pointing towards the faucet, big and hard.

"My, God, Jack. It's actually dripping!"

I watched as pre-cum gathered at the tip and drooled down.

"Well,"I said. "Well."

She knelt down and took me in her mouth. She worked my shaft and swirled her tongue over my head. It was so good my knees actually trembled.

She stood up. "God, Jack. Is this really making you that horny?"

It was a moment of truth time. I could deny it, and have it be an obvious lie. My pecker was bobbing, after all. Or I could admit it.

"I guess so." A couple of hours ago, before I had seen my lips, I never would have admitted to such a thing. But now…now I was a changed man. the world was opening up for me as it had never opened before.

"Well," she said. "Have a seat and let me get to work. Jenny's going to come back in a while, and I want to at least show her some progress."

Molly sat next to me at her vanity table and fitted fake nails to my digits. I don't have the gnarly mitts of people who work with machines and tools. In fact, one of my hobbies is music. Playing the guitar and the piano, and my fingers reflect that. They are long and slender. And now they grew longer and more slender.

Molly pushed the cuticles, trimmed and sanded. She selected some modest ovals for my first time nails, and put a dab of glue on the backs to help the natural adhesive they came with.

"These have to last a week, and I don't want you losing them," she explained.

Long lasting lipstain, long lasting nails…my wife really had this planned out.

I had never realized how delicate and intricate the hand motions required to apply make up were. I watched as she stroked down from the cuticle. Several strokes, and my nails were red. Blood red. To match my lips.

She did the next nail, and the next. She was surprisingly fast for such delicate work.

Then she put on another coat, and another.

"Three strokes down and three coats on," she mumbled, almost like a catechism. Then she put on a clear coat to preserve and protect.

"All right," she smiled happily. "These puppies will last. Get your feet up here."

"My feet?"

"They'll look so delicious, pointing out from your open toed high heels."

She had an almost evil grin on her face when she said that, and I put my feet up.

She didn't have to put fake nails on my toes, although she laughed and threatened me with them. But it did take a bit of work. Men's toenails tend to be a bit gnarly. But that just made them look super good when they were done.

"Wow!" I exclaimed. I was holding my thigh and lifting my foot so I could see them.

"Sexy, baby." She said. "Now stop admiring yourself and let me do your face."

I sat still and she leaned into me, her face close, her breath on my flesh, and began cleaning my pores. She scrubbed me clean with moisturizer, then began putting on primer. As she worked she offered explanations. "The primer makes your face a little flat, takes the color out. Makes your face into a canvas."

"So you're going to paint a picture on my face."

"Your face is going to be a picture, all right. Maybe I'll put a moo cow on your forehead. Or a birdie flying across your cheek."

"Haven't you done enough?"

"Not nearly," and she giggled. "This is foundation, gets rid of any blemishes…which you don't have. You have extremely excellent skin. We should have done this long ago."

"Why didn't you?"

"I thought about it."

That surprised me. "Really?"

"Oh, yes. Haven't you ever wondered why I make you wear your hair long? I dream of making you up and brushing your hair out, giving you a few curls…this is blush. See the color coming back?"

I could, and I said so.

"Now, the eyes. This is the delicate part. Do you want dark, smoky eyes? Or blue eyes? Or shiny eyes? What do you think is sexy?"

"Shadowy."

"Ooh. I like shadows. I'l make it look like your eyes are in caves. Staring out at the world like a dangerous animal."

Her words made me shiver and my cock bob. She laughed.

"Speaking of dangerous animals."

"Crap. I just came yesterday."

"Wait until I'm done with you. You'll be a walking cum machine. You'll spew like the world is ending."

"I think it may—"

"Honey! I'm home!" Jenny's voice drifted back to us.

Molly giggled. "What a clown," she observed, then she yelled, "Back here!"

Jenny entered the room. Tom was right behind her.

"Holy fuck!" Jenny whispered.

"My God," Tom blurted. "Your face, it's just like…just like…"

"Like a girl's," Molly spoke with satisfaction. "I told you I'm good."

"And look, his…" Jenny stopped talking. And her silence was so loud we turned and looked at her.

She was staring at my penis. Red and big and hungry, drooling, bobbing, wanting.

Molly snickered. "Told you he was big."

"Yeah, but…but…"

"Hey, babe," Tom interjected.

She looked up at him. She looked at Molly. She looked at my dick. I might not have even existed, except for my penis and, of course, the fact that I was gaining a woman's face.

She grabbed Tom and turned him around. "You and I have to talk." Her voice was actually fierce, and she walked him out of the room.

"What the heck?" I murmured.

Molly just smiled.

"Come on. Let's put some earrings on you, and some rings and bangles and stuff."

She chose a pair of medium size rings and she took out a needle and a little bottle.

"What are you doing?"

"Piercing." she examined my lobe, handled it and put the needle to it.

"I don't think—OW!"

"Shut up. You'll thank me."

Well, it didn't look like I had much choice. She pierced my other ear and set the earrings in place.

It felt weird, having the danglies caressing the side of my neck, but cool, too.

"Let's put a bone through your nose and we'll be done."

I looked at her. "No."

She grinned. "No. Maybe some other time."

"Maybe some other life."

"Ooh, did you just propose to me for another lifetime?"

I bumbled on an answer for that one, and she took my hand and dragged me out to the living room.

Tom and Jenny were sitting on the couch, facing each other, and in very close consultation. Their faces were two inches apart, and it looked like they had been discussing matters of deep import. They looked at us when we entered, and Jenny turned back to Tom. “Well?”

He sighed. Looked at me. He looked back at his wife. He almost seemed to sag as he nodded and said, “Yes.”

Jenny hugged him, and planted a big smackeroo on his mouth. “You’ll be so glad.”

“I think it’s you who will be glad,” he quipped.

I wondered what they had been talking about.

“Let’s dress him,” stated Molly.

Jenny clapped her hands and jumped up. “Wait until you see what we got him.”

I took notice of the bags then. There were a lot of them. “What’d you do? Buy the store out?”

“Don’t you worry your pretty head about that,” Jenny gushed. “I’m frugal, and I know my way around a sale.”

“Oh.”

“Doesn’t he need a wig? Or something?”

The girls stood back and inspected me.

“We could try combing his hair out. It might be long enough.”

“Long enough for a bob. Tom, go get my wig from the closet. And in the garage there’s a foot square box. It’s marked ‘Aunt.’ Bring that, too.”

Tom stood up. He had the most interesting expression on his face. Sort of an anticipation, when he looked at me. “Okay.”

Tom gone they stripped me. All the way. Not that a peignoir is much. I stood there, a slender man with a woman’s face, and my cock was hard and erect and pointing and…God, was I horny.

Jenny grabbed my penis, looked down at it, and sounded like she was ready for a ten course meal. “We’re going to need to do something about this.”

“We?” asked Molly, a twisted grin on her face.

“Well…well…” Jenny licked her lips, then reluctantly let go of my penis.

They put a pair of panties on me, and that sure didn’t work. My cock was so hard it nearly ripped the material.

“How about the corset?” Jenny asked.

“Too short.”

“I’ve got a longer one.”

At that moment Tom came back in. He was carrying the wig and a box and he put them down.

"Honey, go get my corset, the boned one, in my top drawer."

Tom nodded. He was being a good sport, just going along with it, and I wondered why. Something was not right here.

"Okay, let's put this bra on him."

Jenny took a large cupped bit of cloth out of a bag and held it out. Together they wrapped it around me, fastened it, adjusted it, and pulled it up over my shoulders.

"Now this is a real over the shoulder boulder holder," Molly giggled. "How are we going to fill this?"

Jenny went to the box, opened it and reached in. "Voila!" she bragged, and lifted a pair of breast forms up.

"Oh, my Gosh!" marveled Molly. "Where on earth?"

"My aunt had a mastectomy. Left these to remember her by."

"Well, bless your aunt."

"Bless indeed. Now, come here, sexy."

The way she called me sexy, it was…more. That's all I can say. There was something going on with Jenny. She was flustered and excited and everything, and more than just a simple make over should be. Even if I was that make over.

She shoved the big mounds into my cups, and suddenly I had a monster build. Like I say, I'm slender, except for my big belly, of course. But Tom chose that moment to arrive with the longer corset.

"Holy, fuck!" he whispered. "That's really…really.."

"Pull your tongue in, lover. She's not for you."

Molly glanced at Jenny, and there was something really significant in that glance. I didn't understand, but Molly seemed to, and she seemed to be having deep thoughts.

"Here we go," they helped me step into the garment and pulled it up. When they reached my weenie it was tough going. My pogo stick didn't want to stop jumping. Still, they pulled, and pushed, and told me to suck it in, and they managed to get the corset on me. It had a snap at the bottom and they snapped it up so I couldn't dangle, should I ever get soft.

My cock, of course, was pointed up, and I was pooched a little bit over. It hurt a little, but I could stand it.

Then came the nylons and the dress, and, finally, the high heels.

And the wig.

Done.

They put me in front of a mirror and I gasped. As well as I could considering the corset.

I was a tall woman with an hourglass shape. And a lot of hours topside.

My calves were made shapely by the high heels, and as long as I didn't try to walk I was okay. Not going to fall on my face.

My ass and my chest were flared out, courtesy of the corset, which made my hips round and my chest…you know about my chest.

Then the face. Delicately made up, shaded so the strong masculine lines of my chin were softened and rounded.

My eyes were, as she had promised, like glints in a sexy cave.

And everything was topped off by an auburn wig, long tresses waved over my shoulders.

And I knew why women get dressed up. Aside form the sexy feeling of compression, it was a turn on.

"Wow," I blurted.

"Tom, take our picture."

Tom took her cell phone and snapped pics of us. Me in the center, Molly and Jenny by my sides. I bent my knees slightly and we were all pretty much the same size.

We smiled. We aped. We had a ball. And I felt like I was…let loose. Like I had been in prison all my life, and was suddenly set free, and handed a million dollars to boot.

"Tom, go get some champagne," commanded Jenny. " Good champagne."

Dutifully, Tom headed for the liquor store.

Hunh. Why was he being so accommodating? And why was Jenny acting so weird?

But I didn't have a chance to think anymore because of a knock on the door.

We all looked at each other. I was suddenly frightened, but the girls pushed me towards the door, and I felt a profound sense of…of righteousness. I opened the door, and gaped.

Reverend Thompson stood, bible in hand, and smiled.

Reverend Thompson is old. 80 years old, and his eyesight was fading. He said, "Hi, are Molly and Jack here?"

I was flustered, started blubbering, and Molly pushed past me.

"Hi, Reverend," she stepped out and closed the door. I could hear them talking. Very pleasant.

Jenny turned to me. She held my biceps and focused her gaze on me. It was a hungry gaze and it made me nervous. "Alone at last."

She fused her body to mine. Crushed my lips with hers. I felt one of her hands go to one of my boobs. I knew she was squeezing, feeling, taking advantage of me.

"Hey, wait…I…Molly!"

She laughed, then turned serious. "Jack, I'm going to fuck your brains out. I have never been so turned on in my life. I talked to Tom and he said it's all right. This once, because you're a girl."

"But I…I…"

The door opened and Molly came back in. And stopped. And stared at us.

"Jack?" her voice was level.

I looked at her. "I didn't…she…"

Jenny said: "Molly. I am going to fuck Jack's brains out. When I am done he is going to have a bad case of the stupids."

A long minute passed. Well, it was only seconds, but it felt like minutes. Then: "Oh, is that all."

I gawped at her.

"I thought it was something serious."

"But…but…"

They both giggled, and Molly said, "Jack, I've told you that Jenny is a slut. And she told me earlier that she was going to have your cock in her or else. Well, what could I do? Right?"

"But, Tom…he…"

Tom pushed through the door at that moment. He stopped, didn't even close the door, just stared at Jenny, her arms around me, the look on Jenny and Molly's face. The look on mine.

"What's this…are you trying to fuck my wife?" His voice rose up in anger.

"But…I wasn't…"

He grinned. "Gotcha." Then he grew serious. "Only one thing, Jack."

"Uh…"

"Not in her butt. She hasn't given that to me, yet, and it's sort of reserved, if you get my drift. In fact, she promised me that if I let her fuck you then she'll fuck me. With her asshole. So…you got to do it, man."

"But…but…"

"That's right. No butt."

He and Jenny and Molly laughed then, and Molly pushed me, and Jenny guided me, and I staggered back towards the bedroom.

I've had women before. I'm not one of these guys who never had sex before marriage. In fact, I had had a LOT of sex before being married. But I had never had sex like this.

She walked me into my bedroom and closed the door. She lifted my dress, somehow managed to easily unsnap the bottom of the corset. She rolled the lip of the corset up and managed to extricate my dick.

"But, Jenny, I don't think—"

"Shush," she said. "I'm a slut, I'm in heat, and I've never had a woman."

"But…"

She kissed me. My dick was pressed into her belly, aching and throbbing and drooling.

Her mouth searched mine, our lips were as if glued together, and her tongue explored my mouth. She had her hands on my cheeks at first, then she simply grabbed my earrings and held me in place while she raped my mouth.

Oh, God, was it good! I hadn't kissed another woman than my wife for ten years, and now, to have my mouth savaged by such an expert, it was wonderful, and tender, and different and exciting.

And I thought: *I'm a woman. I...how do I act?*

But I didn't have to worry about how I was supposed to act, Jenny took care of it all for me. She took charge, pushed me back on the bed, mounted me, and I felt my cock engulfed by strange pussy.

Wonderful pussy. So soft, so engulfing. I was surrounded by her womanly flesh and could hardly breath, and it wasn't just the corset. It was the breathlessness of unbridled sex with a stranger.

Not a stranger, but she felt like a stranger. A different person.

"God, you are big," she murmured, bracing her hands on my fake chest, squeezing her hands over my mounds, bending forward to kiss me.

She began to move then, corkscrewing up and down over my shaft. Her hips tilting and pulling, settling down and doing it all over again.

"Oh, fuck!" I whispered, then I realized something. "I don't think I can cum. I just came yesterday."

"That's okay," she breathed, reaching down and fiddling with my balls. My balls that couldn't squirt. "This is for me, not you."

I laughed then. I liked the idea of being used. Of being screwed and tossed aside. And she thought she was the slut!

For long minutes she straddled me, pumping up and down, moaning, groaning, sighing and whining, and, finally, she started to climb the mountain. Her hips started to jerk, and I knew she was cumming.

"Oh, yeah....yes..." she held on to me, her pelvis twitching, then spasming. Then she collapsed, and whispered in my ear, "There is nothing like screwing a woman, is there?"

"No," I whispered back.

At that moment the door burst open and Molly and Tom burst in. They had been listening at the door and had heard Jenny climb the mountain and fall over the other side.

"Aw right! What the fuck is going on!"

"Fuck is going on!" snapped Tom, savage but grinning.

"And nobody asked us to partake. Can you believe these selfish oafs?"

"Oafs," agreed Tom. "Selfish!"

"Well, there's only one way to handle sex oafs."

She bent and opened the bottom drawer of her dresser.

Jenny sat up, curious, "What's that?"

Molly stood up and was holding a mess of straps and a dildo. A...

dildo?

I goggled as she put it on. "Jack, when I first came up with the idea of feminizing you I realized there was one thing we would have to do."

"Have to," agreed Jenny, giggling.

"Damn, dude," said Tom. "Or maybe I should say dudette."

Molly stood, legs spread, a big cock sprouting from her groin. "What do you say, Jack? Are you going to go all the way? Or have I wasted my time with you."

Jenny turned to me. "Yeah, Jack. Are you going to put out? Or are you just a bitch?"

I was speechless.

"Tom," commanded Molly. "There's a big jar of lube in the bathroom. Get it."

Tom moved to obey. He came back in the room and handed the jar to Molly. He was grinning like his face was going to split apart. "I always wondered about this. If you do it…I'll do it. Okay, Jack?"

I was caught. I was unable to speak. I couldn't believe it. The three just stood there and stared at me expectantly.

So what could I do?

I turned over and got on all fours.

"Oh, goody," mumbled Jenny. "Give me that jar. Lube yourself up."

I could hear Tom saying, "here, let me do that, and knew that he was stroking her cock, maybe even kissing her. I felt Jenny's fingers working between my crack, feeling slick, and then she was lubing me. Pushing lube into my rectum. Reaming me with her fingers.

"Oh, fuck!" I moaned. I had never felt anything so good. It felt even better than fucking. Now how could that be?

"Okay, Jack. Tome to be a woman." Molly moved between my legs. Jenny spun around on the bed and faced me. She watched my face as Molly touched her prick to my button.

"Oh, yeah," Jenny smiled as my face opened up.

I felt that penis go deep into me. I had no breath, but what was left was snatched away. I perched on the precipice of a giant dick and my world was totally and utterly blown.

She pulled back and it felt like somebody was turning me inside out.

"Wow," muttered Tom. His voice was filled with awe and jealousy.

She thrust into me, forced me forward, and Jenny chose that moment to kiss me. There I knelt, on all fours, a hard penis pushing me forward and a soft kiss stopping me. I had never imagined anything could feel this good in my life.

In and out, and my back started scrunching up, then flattening out, I pushed my butt back and twisted, giving her penis a corkscrew of a fuck.

"Oh, baby, this is good," Molly mumbled.

I looked back over my shoulder, and her face was twisted in lust, and I understood something. She was taking my male power. She was absorbing that which made me a man, and that was okay. I certainly didn't mind a wife that pounded me with her pecker, who made me feel this way. Heck, I had made her feel this way for a decade, and what was sauce for the gander is sauce for the goose.

"Oh, my God! Look!" I intuited that Tom was pointing, and Jenny looked, then lowered my head so I could see between my arms, and back to where my dick hung.

White sperm was seeping out of Mr. Happy. I was cumming. I wasn't having an orgasm, but it felt good, happy, loosy goosy, and I was being milked. Her cock was pressing on my prostate and semen was being forced out of me.

And this was okay. I couldn't cum anyway, and this warm feeling... I had an idea it was going to last for days. The cum without a cum.

Jenny lifted my face and kissed me some more. Molly slowed down and just held her position and waited for me to empty out.

"He's done," announced Tom, and she pulled slowly out.

"Oh, God!" I said, and I fell forward, sated, but not exhausted. In fact, I had never felt so alive in my life. I was wired with sex and happiness and an inner glow.

"Well, good," Molly slapped my ass. "Now we should—"

"Ahem."

The girls looked at Tom.

Jenny said, "Really?"

Molly asked, "What?"

Jenny: "He wants to screw Jack."

"Really?"

"Really. He's been trying to get me to do anal for years, and now, seeing this beautiful ass, and if Jack is willing..."

I lay there. Was I willing? I had been made into a woman, and fucked by another woman, and then fucked by a woman made into a man, sexually. So, was I willing? Could I take yet another step?

Molly slithered up next to me, turned my face towards her.

"Jack, if you don't want to I understand. But this is your friend, and you just had his wife, and I'm going to be fucking you all week long, and maybe Jenny will to—"

"I will."

"But...if you want to try it...it won't be any harder than my dick, and it will be real flesh. Would you like to experience real flesh, Jack?"

Oh, God. What could I do? What could I say? These were my friends, and they meant so much to me. I struggled to my hands and knees and waited.

END

A Note from the Author!

I hope you liked these little tales.
Please take a moment to rate me five stars.
That helps support my writing,
and lets me know which direction I should take
for future books.

HAVE A HORNY DAY!

Grace

About the Author!

Grace Mansfield is the cutting edge of feminization in modern society.

Grace writes an astounding 10,000 words a day, and her five star ratings are out the roof!

That's over a hundred novels and over 600 novellas, and in just a couple of years!

But feminization isn't her only thing. She writes stories about female domination, chastity, crossdressing, femdom, even castration!

She explores themes that others have never touched upon!

She explores human beings and all their blessings and foibles.

She ranges far in her plotting, so you'll never get the same old same old.

If you really want the absolute best in erotica check her out on Amazon.

Or, just drop on by the website.

Joe Gropper
Webmaster at
https://gropperpress.wordpress.com

THERE ARE TWENTY-ONE

21 STORY BUNDLES!

for a massive collection of bundles!

On Amazon type in:

'GRACE MANSFIELD 21 STORIES'

21 steamy five star stories in each bundle!

All focusing on Feminization, Female Domination, chastity, spanking, BDSM, pegging, and more!

Type in…

'GRACE MANSFIELD 21 STORIES'

THE 21 STORY BUNDLES!

A massive collection of bundles!

21 steamy five star stories in each book!

All focusing on Feminization, Female Domination, chastity, spanking, BDSM, pegging, and more!

Available on Amazon!

Or go to:
https://gropperpress.wordpress.com

THE BEST OF GRACE MANSFIELD?

each bundle has
15 steamy five star stories
PLUS a complete novel!

Available on Amazon!

Five
Sizzling
Stories!
Five
Sizzling
Stories!
Five
Sizzling
Stories!
Volume Three
The Castration Chronicles!
Stories of emasculation,
feminization and castration!
Go to Amazon:
The Castration
Chronicles!

Full Length Books!

ROD tricks his wife by locking a vibrator to her vaginal piercings. She's at a ladies camp and he's at a campground a mile away, playing with his fob and causing her hilarious torment. But she who laughs last…!

Feminized at a Lesbian Summer Camp!

Available on Amazon!

Or go to:

https://gropperpress.wordpress.com

A Tour de Force!

Roscoe was a power player in Hollywood. He was handsome, adored, and had one fault - he liked to play practical jokes. Now his wife is playing one on him, and it's going to be the grandest practical joke of all time.

I Changed My Husband into a Woman

Kindle customers said: Told first-person by loving but vengeful wife of rich cheating husband…Excellent read for forced-fem lovers…the deflowering was perfect.

Here are the first two chapters from…

Sissy Ride: The Book

PART ONE

My name is Alex Trenton, and I didn't mean for it to happen. In fact, even though I took the first step, I am not responsible. I am the victim here.

I was sitting at my computer, it was a Tuesday night. I had a bourbon and Coke I was sipping, and enjoying very greatly, and I was surfing porn.

I know, me bad, but Tanya, my wife, was at a convention for the week. I was all alone, and…and I was sitting there in my bathrobe, stroking my hog, getting all excited over the babes I was looking at.

Big breasts heaving, while some big-dicked stud plowed them.

Some cock tunneling between big breasts and shooting cream all over the delightful flesh.

Or, my favorite, big breasted woman on all fours, jerking back and forth, facing the camera so I could see those enormous hooters and those red, red lips.

Money shot after money shot, squirting over buttocks, boobs, gorgeous faces, and I was ready to shoot my own load.

DING! The box flashed up on my screen. I had a message.

I started to delete it and stopped. It was from…Mistress Mandy?

Mistress Mandy? Who the hell was that?

I didn't recognize the name, but there was this little round picture of, get this, red lips, on the message.

I love red lips. And I know I shouldn't have done it, you're not supposed to open anything you don't know on the web, I opened it.

The message read:

I saw you the other day and knew.
You are the perfect man.
I've been stalking you.
I want you to do something for me.

I blinked. Stalking? Out of the blue?

I went over all the women I had met over the past few weeks.

There were women at work. There were women on the street and in stores. But who, what woman, would pick a guy out at random and stalk him?

DING!

Please do something for me.
You have to.
I'll die if you don't.

She'd die? What the heck?

Merely a figure of speech. No intention.

But it was powerful, made me notice, made me not delete and block.

I typed:

Who is this?

I sat back, sipped a bit of bourbon, and wondered.

Was it Marsha? That secretary at the office? I had flirted with her, but she knew I was married.

Or maybe some clerk at the grocery store. Maybe some young thing bagged for me, and now wanted to…'bag' me.

My thoughts and fantasies were interrupted by…

DING!

It doesn't matter.
I just know that you like porn,
and that we have the same tastes.

She knew my tastes? Maybe it was just a random porn advertisement, searching for a sucker.

No. There had been no request for money. The internet always wants your money.

I typed:

What do you know about me?

I sure hoped some Russian hairball wasn't sitting over in Moscow, drinking vodka and chuckling and thinking, 'I got a bite!'

DING!

I know you like big titted girls getting it doggy style.
I know you're fascinated by men with breasts.
I know you look at all the sites
where men are dominated by woman.
I know you've had a deep interest
in meeting a mistress
who will take you where you want to go.

It was off the internet. Only somebody on the internet would know what I liked to surf.

DING!

Watch this!

A simple link. Did I dare click on it? What could it hurt? I wouldn't get a virus unless I clicked on something on the site, just looking at something wasn't going to hurt.

I clicked on the link.

A window opened, a title page, and I just about dropped my jaw all the way to the floor.

Mommy Compilation part four!

Casca and Ryan and…and all the other big titted mothers I had seen again and again. It was one of my favorites, but how had this 'mystery messenger', this 'Mistress Mandy,' known?

And I knew she, I hoped it was a she, was into my computer history.

And she wouldn't even have to crack my computer. All she had to do was hack into my Google history, or some other source.

I was actually sweating at this point.

DING!

I need you to do something for me.
You'll like it.

I'd like it? I'd like what?

And I was scared, but I was also so mind fucked that I didn't know what to do.

I was being stalked.

But it was sex.

And I was drunk and horny.

I hadn't gotten any for a week. My wife was away.

I stared as some cock exploded the white stuff all over Casca's titties on the screen. Possibly the most perfect tits in the history of the world.

I looked down at my lap. I was stroking myself. I had stopped when the messages started, but somewhere along the road I had started stroking again. Probably when the Mommy Compilation opened up.

And I knew, it was the idea of the secret stalker. It was somebody, who I didn't know at all, sending me sexy messages.

I typed:

What do you want me to do?

DING!

Put on your wife's clothes.

What!?

I typed:

You're kidding.

DING!

She'll have a bra. Put it on.
Do you have condoms?

I didn't want to answer, but I was compelled. This was getting too weird.

But it was a fantasy I had always had. Putting on a woman's clothes. I had read every entry on Literotica about cross dressers.

Just the thought was making my boner even more erect.

I looked down at my lap. There was a drop of pre-cum sliding out of the head of my cock.

I typed:

I have condoms.

DING!

Do it.
Now.
Please.

I couldn't bring myself to move.

I typed:

This is too weird.

DING!

I'm not asking you to cheat.
I just want you to enjoy yourself.
To do what you want to do.
Where's the harm?

I typed:

Who are you?

DING!

You'll never know if you don't
put on that bra.
Put water in the condoms.
Place the condoms in the bra.

I sat there. I sipped. My dick was getting harder. I was close to cumming, but I didn't want to cum. If I came I would lose my sexual urgency, and I wanted to keep it high.

I wanted to put that damned bra on.

I wanted to have tits, no matter how fake.

DING!

Please.

I typed:

What do you get out of it?

DING!

When I know that you are wearing that bra I will jill off.
that is my reward for helping you.

It was a woman. She had said 'Jill off' instead of 'Jack off.'

But her reward was for helping me?

I typed:

Helping me?

DING!

Helping you find the truth of yourself.
Helping you give in to your secret urges.
Helping you realize that it's okay…
to be a woman.

I stared at the words on the screen. I felt like I was apart from my body, and there was a faint scream way back in the basement of my skull.

I had never thought about being a woman.

But seeing these words on the computer, putting that together with the things I watched on the internet, the porn I read…did I want to try it?

Did this 'phantom messenger' know something about me that I didn't know? That I needed to know?

I typed:

I'll do it.

Before I was out of the swivel chair my screen dinged:

HURRY!

Fuck! I thought. What was I doing? What would Tanya think? I knew this was definitely beyond the limits of our relationship.

But it wasn't like I was cheating. I was just…a little horny.

I'd do this, wack off, and see if I liked it.

I didn't think about what would happen if I did like it.

I walked down the hall to my bedroom. I opened my wife's drawer, then closed it. She would notice if I used something all folded and neat.

I went into the bathroom and looked in the hamper.

Bingo. A pink bra, and it looked like it was well worn, a little stretched.

I tried to put it on and couldn't. Damned thing was weird. And I couldn't reach up behind myself and fasten the clasps like I had seen Tanya do so easily.

Then I remembered. I had seen her method. I pulled it around my stomach and fastened it and then pulled it so the cups were in front and… cripes! The thing was inside out or something.

Of course. I mentally figured out the proper procedure, put the cups the right way, fastened it, pulled it around, and bingo. I was wearing her bra.

It was a little tight. She was more narrow than I. But not that tight.

And the boobs, thank God, were big. I'm one of those lucky guys that had a wife with big boobs.

I went into the bathroom and looked in a mirror.

A guy with a bra. Not sexy. But then why was my peter bouncing like a puppet on strings?

I returned to the bedroom and got out two condoms. The nozzle in the bathroom wouldn't work, so I had to walk through the house. The curtains were closed, but it felt so weird, and kinky, and my dick was really enjoying this. I actually dripped some pre-cum on the hallway floor.

The kitchen sink wouldn't work.

I went into the garage, and the laundry sink worked. I put the condoms over the nozzle and watched while they grew bigger.

How big is a boob? Especially when it is fake and about to be put into a bra like the one I was wearing?

I liked big boobs, so I let the water build up, and the condom grew bigger and hung down, and I stopped and tied it off.

I filled the other condom, trying to make sure they were the same size.

I put them in my bra.

'My' bra. Not Tanya's. In some weird way I had fashioned ownership over her lingerie.

I walked back through the house, now bouncing and jiggling.

God, it felt good, and I left more pre-cum splatters on the floor. I was really leaking now.

I looked into the mirror.

A man with boobs. Fuck!

I went back to the computer.

I typed:

I did it.

DING!

What's it like?

I typed:

Weird. Sexy.

DING!

Are you hard?

I didn't even think about how bizarre this was. I was now officially too horny to think straight.

I typed.

I'm really fucking hard.

DING!

Good.
Don't jack off, yet.

I typed.

Why not?

DING!

I want you to do something else.

I typed:

What?

Now I realized that I was into the game. Heysoos! What was happening to me? But I was too horny to stop.

DING!

Put on a blouse, or sweater, or something
that will really show your boobs off.

I typed:

I'll do it.

DING!

HURRY!

I got up and went back to the bedroom. I went through my wife's closet. Blouses were so thin my bra would be too visible, the fakery would be too easily seen.

Sweaters were too tight. I was afraid I would stretch them out.

A jacket? I had visions of myself, stacked, showing cleavage through the open front. But, no.

Then I saw the dress.

Fuck! A dress? The Mystery Messenger had said a shirt, but I didn't think she would complain if I put on a dress.

It was purple. Just a little loose at the neck. Stretchy. It wouldn't get all pulled out of shape.

I took it off the hanger and held it up.

Right size.

I put it on.

Oh, God! I thought I was going to cum right there! Then I realized something. I was dripping so much I was going to leave stains.

Quickly, I lifted up the dress and looked around.

Damn! What would a woman do it she had a cock that was dripping…then I laughed. A hard bark. I was imagining really strange things.

Then I realized the solution.

Still holding my dress up I went to the hamper and pulled out undies. Panties. A match for the bra I had on.

I put the panties on, then opened a drawer under the sink and pulled out a Kotex.

I put it in the panties where my dick would drip, and pulled the panties up. I let my dress down.

'My' dress.

And realized I had gone too far. The Mystery Messenger, Mistress Mandy, 'MM' I would think of her from here on out, had only said a shirt. But now I had on a dress and panties. And…a Kotex.

Which thought made my dick surge so hard I was afraid I was going to cum in my panties.

Could the panty liner catch a load of sperm? I didn't think so.

I quickly fumbled up the dress, reached into my panties and squeezed my cock. Hard. I waited, and slowly the urge to squirt faded.

Sighing, I went to the kitchen, poured another drink, then went back to the computer.

I typed:

Couldn't find a blouse.

No response.

I typed:

I put on a dress.
Is that okay?

DING!

Wow!
Perfect.
How do you feel?

Truthfully, I typed:

I almost came in my panties.

DING!

You're wearing panties?

I typed:

I had to.
I was dripping.
I needed a panty liner.

Nothing for a while. I started the Mommy Compilation video over again.

I watched those big breasts bounce and sway as men ground into women, and I felt…proud? Happy?

I had my own set of tits!

Whoever this MM was…she had called me rightly. There was something so horny and intoxicating about wearing woman's clothes.

DING!

Lipstick.

My mind just sort of popped. The only thing that kept me from passing out was the fact that I was sedated by whiskey.

I typed:

What?

DING!

You know you want to.

I typed:

No.
I don't.
I can't do that.

DING!

I can see you in my mind's eye.
Sitting there so sexy.
Your big boobs overflowing.
I can see you with long hair,
all curled and wavy.
I can see your face,
perfectly made up.
But,
most of all,
I can see your lips.
Your red, red lips.
Does your wife have red lipstick?
Really red lipstick?

I didn't sip now, I gulped. I needed the liquid courage.

Putting on lipstick? That would be like the final line to cross!

That was so far out there I didn't think I could do it!

I gulped again.

DING!

For me?
Please?
I need to see you in my mind's eye.
I need to know your lips are sexy red.
Blow job red.
Red enough for me to kiss and kiss.
Can you imagine me kissing your red lips?
Can you?

I could. Oh, my God, I could. I could see my lips, round and red and waiting to be kissed.

The drinks hitting me harder, I typed:

I'll do it.

DING!

HURRY!

I ran, actually ran, to the bedroom, to the back bathroom. I opened the medicine cabinet. Nothing there.

Then I realized I was drunk and not thinking. My wife wouldn't leave her lipstick in the medicine cabinet, especially when she had a make up table.

I went to her table, and there, sitting to the side, all by itself, almost like it wanted to be noticed, was a thin, gold tube.

I sat down and opened the tube. It wasn't the roll on stuff, but a little applicator.

I puckered my lips at the mirror and began painting.

One coat made them red. Two coats filled in the cracks. Three coats. I wanted this to be perfect.

They were. Beautiful, luscious red. A light metallic sheen to them. And they looked plumper. I looked at the tube.

BUXOM
Lip stain and plumper

Lip stain? A dull thought shot through me. What was the difference between lip stain and lipstick?

Still, nothing connected.

I stared in the mirror for a long time. My lips were larger, so that was what the plumper was. And I was so-o-o sexy.

Big boobs. Red lips.

I stood up.

I wasn't big boned, but I could use a corset or something. Still, though I was a bit angular, I was so fucking turned on I couldn't believe it.

I picked up my glass and took a sip. There was only the lightest trace of lipstick on the glass. It must have dried fast.

I went back to the computer room. I sashayed through the house. I sauntered through the rooms.

My chest swayed, and I tried to put some sway into my ass. And I got an idea. Heels.

I had often admired how my wife's ass swayed when she wore heels.

I returned to the bedroom and searched my wife's closet.

In the back, a pair of three inch stiletto heels. She never wore them anymore. They had open toes and a sling on the heel.

I put them on, and barely fit. My toes stretched the front strap, and the heel strap, but I managed to stand in them.

I was shaky, had to work to keep my balance, especially with all the liquor I had been drinking.

I stood for a long moment, just practicing standing, and I saw it. On the top shelf, in the back of the closet, was a box. My wife's wig. She hadn't worn it for ages. Had only bought it for one occasion, a bad hair cut.

I took the box down and opened it. A blonde wig. Long and curly.

I tried to remember how she had put it on, and fitted it to my head. It took a while, but I managed.

I walked out of the closet. Red lips, big tits, long hair, and my ass swaying like it was a hammock.

Fuck!

And my dick was pushing my panties out and spoiling the look of the dress.

I returned to the computer room.

MM had left another message.

Where are you?

I sat down and typed:

I couldn't help it.
I couldn't stop myself.

DING!

What did you do?

I typed:

I put on the lipstick, then I put on high heels.
I even put on my wife's wig.

DING!

Oh, God!
My pussy is throbbing!
I want to see you!

Even drunk, I thought, *no way!*
I typed:

No way!

DING!

Well,
take a picture for yourself.
Take a few pictures.
You're going to want to remember this always.

I typed:

I will.

DING!

I need to cum now.

I thought about this. In my addled state I wondered. Is jacking off at the same time cheating? Did I dare?

Of course I dare. I was drunk and horny and I needed to squirt in the worst possible way.

I typed:

Me, too.

DING!

We need to cum at the same time.

I typed:

How do we work this?

DING!

Stroke yourself,
at the end of one minute cum.
I will do the same.

The idea of cuming together, separately, was erotic, and I lifted my dress out of the way and grabbed my cock.

DING!

Look at your computer.

Computers have the same time.
Get your message ready,
just say 'now!'
send it when your minute changes.
When the minute changes again we cum.

I took a quick sip, prepared my message, and watched the digital clock on my computer.

The numbers changed. I sent the message, and began stroking.

Oh, God! It felt good, within ten seconds I was holding myself back.

I could imagine her, whoever she was, diddling her pussy. Maybe using a dildo, definitely a vibrator.

She would be playing with her tits, maybe even sucking a nipple.

I wanted to suck my own nipples.

I fondled my balls.

I stroked.

Time passed, I was on the edge…on the edge…

The number changed.

"OH…OHHHH! Oh! Oh!"

Semen spurted across the room. A long rope of sticky, white fluid. My hips locked up and I couldn't move, white heat filled my mind and everything got dim. I had never experienced such an explosive cum in my life!

Then it was done.

I sat for a minute, drained and not wanting to move, but I had to send a message.

I typed:

Was it good?

DING!

God!
Massive!
I'm still feeling little earthquakes inside.

I typed:

Thank you.

DING!

Talk to you later.
Don't forget to take pictures.

I blinked It was like a lifeline had been cut. My whole world had been invested in that messaging. And now it was…over?

I typed:

Wait!
When will we talk again?

No response, and the message window disappeared. She had officially cut the line.

Stunned, satisfied, mystified, I knew I had to take pictures.

I reached into a drawer and took out my good camera. No stupid cell phone for this babe.

I put it on a tripod and set it up in the living room. I used the timer and took a series of pictures. I posed. I kissed at the lens. I flaunted my tits. I never felt so sexy.

And the nice thing, my bump was gone. My boner down, the dress was smooth and not showing any hint of my package.

And then, finally, it was over.

It was time to get undressed and be a man again.

Truth, after I had cum I was ready to change back. I guess that was a good thing. It meant that I just wanted the sex, I didn't want to remain a woman. which shows how people can delude themselves.

Still, I stalled just a bit longer.

I uploaded the pictures to my computer and put them in a file, and I hid the file.

I smiled. Nobody was going to find these puppies.

Then I washed my glass out, odd, the lipstick stain, as light as it was, was very stubborn. Didn't want to come off.

Then I washed a bunch of glasses. They were just sort of dusty, and I imagined myself a woman, just sitting around and doing housework.

Then I washed the cupboards off, cleaned a few more things, and realized the time.

It was two in the morning! And I had been prancing around like a woman for hours! Hunh! Maybe there was a part of me that did want to be a woman.

Then I talked myself out of it.

It was just a one time thing.

I went to the bedroom, thought about sleeping as a woman, then decided against it. I wasn't that horny anymore, though I did have an inner buzz of excitement running through me.

I took off the wig and put it away. I took off the dress and hung it up. I took the water condoms out of the bra and put them in the sink. I didn't pop them, I wanted to wear them again. I probably wouldn't, but...I just left them in the sink.

I took off my panties, and the liner was soaked from the pre cum I had emitted earlier. I smiled at the thought of how much juice I had shot. God, what a night!

Finally, I looked in the mirror at my lipstick. Lip stain. My lips were still plump. This stuff really worked.

I decided to just hop into the shower and wash the stuff off.

I turned the water on hot, hopped in and soaped up.

I rubbed my lips, soaped them good, rubbed them some more, and grinned. I would be clean now.

I got out of the shower, dried myself off, and looked in the mirror.

Oh, no! The lipstick was still there.

I grabbed a washcloth and soaped it up and scrubbed my lips some more.

They stayed red. In fact, because of all the rubbing they were a little redder.

A little worried, I went back to the computer and powered up. I researched lip stain.

Long lasting than lipstick. It doesn't just apply a color over the lips, it stains the skin.

My jaw dropped and I stared at the screen. The site I was on had dozens of red lips on it. Lips on women. Red lips where they should be. Not on a man.

What had I done?

I researched some more. Most stains came off within a day. I looked up the particular brand I had used. Three days. One day to lose most of the color, but three days to lose all the color.

Three days.

It was Wednesday night. That meant Thursday, Friday, and Tanya was due home on Saturday. Saturday afternoon.

Yes. It would work, though there might be a little redness left. but i could talk fast and cross my fingers…it was workable.

But, first, I was going to have to call in sick. I couldn't be seen at work with lips like these.

So I set my alarm and went to sleep.

And woke up late. And my head hurt.

I groaned, rolled over and picked up my cell.

There was a message on it, from Tanya.

Tried to reach you last night.
Where were you?

I was dressing up in your clothes, my love. Why do you ask? I giggled.

I called up work and put on my best fake cough. It was pretty easy, and they bought it. Heck, in this day of COVID the slightest wheeze was an excuse to lock down and quarantine.

I called Tanya then.

"Hey, babe! How you doing?" she greeted me.

"I'm good, but I miss you!" At least I missed you until last night, and then I was a bad boy.

"Oh, I miss you, too. I can't wait to feel your big dick in me."

"Whoa! I like that! Tell me more."

"I couldn't help myself," she giggled. I masturbated last night."

What!? She never did such things. She was the original Miss Goody Two Shoes.

"I can't believe it."

"Believe."

"Well, how was it?"

This talk was turning me on. And I was already turned on by having dressed up the night before, and by looking at my red, red lips this morning.

"Oh, I had a big bang. The kind that just sort of take your breath away and leave you dazed and confused."

"Geez, hearing you talk like that has given me a boner. I'm going to have to jack off."

"Don't you dare! You save it for me! When I get home I'm going to jump your bone seven ways from go."

"Oh, so you can beat off, but I can't?"

"No. You're a man."

"And I have a man's needs."

"You've had your needs filled too often, and you're going to get your needs really filled when I get home. So no jacking off!"

DING!

I stared at the computer screen. MM had sent me a message? Right while I was talking to my wife!

I clicked on the message box.

"Honey? Are you there?"

"Uh, yeah!" My mind was caught between two conversations, I was fumbling the ball.

On the screen:

Hi, lover.
You ready for tonight?

Oh, no!

"Yeah I can't wait to fuck you," I said.

"You sound kind of funny. Is everything all right?"

"Oh, yeah…"

I typed:

Yes.

I said: "I'm just looking forward to making love to you."

DING!

We're really going to go crazy tonight.
Are you ready?

"I'm ready," I said.

"What?"

"What?" I was getting confused.

DING!

We're going to paint your nails
and dress you all the way up.

"You just said you were looking forward to making love, and then you asked 'what.' What's going on?"

DING!

Then you're going to walk around.
Outside.
You're going to be so brave.

I tried to separate the conversations in my head. I pushed the MM aside in my mind, turned my swivel away from the screen, and said.

"Sorry honey, I just cut my finger. Paper cut."

"Are you all right?"

"Oh, yeah. No big deal. And I can't wait to see you."

DING!

I ignored the bell. "I'm going to go crazy on you."

She giggled. "That sounds like fun. But can you handle a real woman?"

As opposed to a computer message woman? "Oh, yeah. I feel like real woman right now." I blinked. Was there something revealing about what I had said?

DING!

"Like the Shania Twain song," she said.

I searched my mind. I didn't want to read messages. Oh, yeah. I remembered the song. I hummed a bit of it.

Tanya sang: "Man, I feel like a woman."

DING!

But now I was successfully in the groove. I put aside the thoughts of the constant messages and focused on my wife.

For a long minute we talked, and even talked dirty, to each other. then it was time to hang up.

DING! DING! DING!

Her last words were, "Well, take care of yourself. You do sound a little strange."

"I'm fine. And I look forward to this weekend so much."

"Me, too. Bye, lover."

I hung up, and I was aware that MM had opened up by calling me 'lover,' and that my wife had hung up calling me 'lover.'

What a tangled web I was in.

I turned to the computer and looked at the messages.

I want you to tell me what you want.

I want to Jill off with you again.

Would you like to put on eye shadow?

In my mind I am kissing you right now.

I'm playing with my pussy, it's hot and wet for you.

I'll talk to you tonight.

This has been the first part of

The Sissy Ride!

Read it on kindle or paperback

Made in United States
Orlando, FL
01 February 2024

43169428R00098